Robert Wallace

Fangs of Murder: Phantom Detective Saga

OK Publishing 2021

Robert Wallace
Fangs of Murder: Phantom Detective Saga

Published by
MUSAICUM
Books

- Advanced Digital Solutions & High-Quality book Formatting -

musaicumbooks@okpublishing.info

2021 OK Publishing

ISBN 978-80-272-7876-3

Contents

Chapter I
Underworld Elections

"You're wanted on the phone, Mr. Ricco. Long distance calling from New York City."

The big, scar-faced man in a flashy bathing suit turned with a scowl of annoyance on the pier where he sat sunning himself over the clear blue waters of Lake Arrowhead.

"Okay, bud," he growled. Getting up, he followed the white-jacketed attendant past other lolling guests of the quiet Adirondack summer resort to a chrome-studded, modernistic bathhouse. Here, in the indicated private booth, he lifted a waiting receiver.

"Yeah?" he demanded.

"This 'Scars' Ricco?" came a voice, at once coarse and yet seeming to hold an acrid, mocking tone.

"Yeah, go ahead!"

"I'm a pal of yours, Scars. Got a little tip for you. Somethin' about what's been doin' here in N.Y. while you're tannin' that beef of yours-somethin' about your mob."

Ricco scowled. But a crafty light showed in his eyes. "Mob?" he echoed naively. "I don't know what you're talking about."

"Cut the stall, Ricco. Just get this! Your mob's taken a powder on you! They've all sold out to Monk Gorman-every one of 'em!"

Ricco's fleshy body stiffened. The diagonal scar on his cheek suddenly stood out, livid. His voice roared.

"Monk Gorman? Why that cheap, nickel-dipping punk ain't got enough dough to buy out —" He broke off, seemed with an effort to steady himself. The scar went dull again as he gave a harsh laugh. "Well, now cut the kiddin'. Who're you and what do you want? You're talkin' to a busy man."

Unheeding this, the voice resumed, "Thought I'd get a rise outa you, Scars. I'm a pal of yours. And listen —"

When Ricco hung up, his scar was livid again. Eyes blazing, he stormed out of the bathhouse —only to burst in again, to grab his clothes.

Fifteen minutes later the stucco, gabled Arrowhead Hotel lost one of its best-paying guests-Scars Ricco, a guest who had been no trouble, kept to his own business, tipped generously. The answer to a management's prayer.

With luggage piled in the rumble seat of his canary-yellow Packard roadster, Ricco drove down the graveled road, out of the rustic gate, and onto the highway for New York.

The big roadster gathered speed as it hurled along with muffler open. It took a long hill, then shot along a level but curved road where white fencing and signposts warned of a sharp, steep embankment. Ricco, his scar livid, hunched over the wheel, mouthing oaths in tune to his fierce thoughts. Before repeal he had controlled the biggest bootleg racket in New York. And he was still a big shot! He still knew how to hold a mob together and-He broke off from his thoughts with a sudden exclamation of alarm. A shadowy shape had closed in swiftly, overtaking him under cover of his exhaust and was now crowding him toward the precipice. He had no time to distinguish it; it was like some Juggernaut bearing down on him.

Ricco's foot left the gas-pedal of his canary roadster. His hand tugged at the wheel. If he felt terror, his throat had no time to express it. For in the next instant there was a brief but jarring impact, the scrape of tortured fenders. There was a kaleidoscopic impression before Ricco's eyes of white fence-posts swinging towards him, parting crazily, flying to both sides.

The careening roadster crashed through the fence, toppled over the embankment. It rolled and rolled, while glass broke and metal snapped groaningly. With a resounding crash the car struck the jagged, stony foot of the cliff-like embankment. Debris mushroomed up, settled —

A pall of dreadful silence remained over the wreck.

In the twisted, broken mass which a moment ago had been a sleek yellow roadster, Scars Ricco sprawled, dead, with broken steering wheel crushed horribly against his ribs, blood drooling from his parted lips.

Above, on the highway to New York, that lunging shadow, a heavy, dark sedan, was shrinking speedily down the macadam, leaving the grim, broken fence far behind.

* * *

At Saratoga, the fifth race was well under way. Dutch Kaltz, comfortably settled in a grand tier box, grinned as he watched, his rubicund face wrinkled in satisfied folds around his Havana cigar.

The horses-thrilling blurs of flying hoofs and huddled jockeys-were coming around to the last stretch.

"Boy, oh boy, whatta race!" chortled Dutch Kaltz, his thick lips caressing the cigar. He turned to his companion, a bored-looking, faded blonde in a flashy green dress. She was stifling a wearied yawn.

"Listen, baby!" he said to her. "If 'Hot Foot' brings home the bacon, I'll get you that new mink coat for the winter."

The blonde came out of her trance with a snap that brought her to the very rail where she promptly shouted with the enthusiasm of a true turf-lover, "Come on, Hot Foot! Come on home-come on, Hot Foot!"

As the horses went into the finish stretch, an usher leaned over the box and slipped a note to Dutch Kaltz.

Annoyed, Kaltz opened it hastily. The cigar dropped from his suddenly gaping mouth. His eyes bulged at the bold, scrawled words:

> Your mob's run out to Monk Gorman. Someone's backing him with dough. Better take this tip from a pal and get busy.

Kaltz's rubicund face looked like a bloated moon. With a snarled oath, he leaped to his feet. Without a word of explanation to his companion, he began moving his shoulder-padded frame toward the exit of the box.

Simultaneously the crowd in the grandstand went wild with cheers. The human din drowned out all other sound. The blonde swept from her chair, yelling joyously as she turned.

"Hot Foot's in, Dutch!" she cried. "Oh Sugar, I can just see myself in that —"

She broke off as she saw Dutch Kaltz's vacated chair. Her eyes flashed with sudden anger across the box, to the exit gate. Then she screamed shrilly, wildly.

The rubicund figure of Dutch Kaltz lay slumped on the floor just beneath the exit. Blood lay in a pool around it. There was a blood-fringed hole in the front of Kaltz's sport coat where the single high-calibred slug had entered, and done its ghastly work. Dutch Kaltz had seen-and run-his last race.

* * *

Indian summer had come to New York City. The night was close and warm. The sky, dull and starless, reflected the bright lights of Manhattan in a vague, ruddy glow.

On a desolate, deserted side street on the lower west side stood a big brick garage which looked as if it had not done business for some time. Its slide-doors were closed, the glass panes covered up so that only dull chinks of light showed through.

But inside, there was sinister life. A crowd of men stood, smoking cigarettes, in various attitudes of attention. The light from naked electric bulbs starkly revealed their hard, coarse-featured faces, their shifty, ever-alert eyes.

"Okay, boys-the whole job's been done! An' without a hitch!"

The harsh voice rasped out in the confines of the garage, the voice of a burly, swart-faced man in a sport-belted slicker. Monk Gorman stood facing the crowd, his hand nestled smugly in a pocket which showed the protecting bulge of an automatic.

"You ain't workin', any of you, for your old bosses-because they just ain't going to be around any more!" he went on triumphantly. "All four of them are washed up, see. Kaltz! Ricco! Flowers Gorsh! And Big Boy Rinaldi!"

There was a grim but awed silence. Thugs who, until this night, had worked for one of those four big king-pins of New York City's underworld, looked impressed rather than regretful. In the unfeeling underworld there was little personal sentiment, especially when money flowed freely.

A broken-nosed man spoke then, with a self-important laugh. "Boy, did I finish Dutch in style! Nobody even heard that silenced gat when I clipped him from the aisle soon as he blew up over that note."

A pallid-faced, long-jawed thug put in, "Hell, Gus, you shoulda seen me sideswipe Ricco over that cliff—"

"Cut it, you mugs!" the big man in the slicker snapped out angrily. Again he addressed the hard-faced gathering.

"Them four babies all got just what was comin' to 'em, see? An' the same goes for anyone else who thinks he's big shot now! Why? Because you're workin' for a guy, bigger than any of these punks ever were! A right guy who won't keep you warmin' park benches while he goes off on vacations! They'll be dough, an' plenty of it! They'll be dough enough to buy the whole damn town! From now on we all got one boss-and we're doin' whatever he tells us, see?"

Eager eyes were fixed on the speaker.

Eager voices rose from the vast interior of the garage.

"Where's th' Big Shot, Monk?"

"Let's meet 'im! Th' dough you jes' passed out from him is like old times!"

"Is he comin' here, Monk?"

"Whadda we do next?"

Monk Gorman again held up his hand for silence.

"I've already told you guys that th' big shot's been-well, he's been sending me orders from where he's been hiding out. Yeah, he's coming to take personal charge tonight-about eleven, when the *Charlemagne* docks. But he ain't coming to this dump."

He paused and indicated the five bullet-riddled bodies which lay in a huddled heap in one corner.

"We've jes' finished our first job for him when we cleaned out Rinaldi's garage here, but we gotta scram. We got one more job to do, and then, if we do it right, we meet th' new Big Shot in person."

Chapter II
Murder by Appointment

Eleven p.m. the clock over the passenger gateway showed the time.

The huge, newly constructed pier on the Hudson River was jammed with people meeting the late docking S.S. *Charlemagne* which was nine hours ahead of its schedule. Private cars and taxis pulled up in turn outside the vast concrete and steel structure which was three city blocks in length.

In a rather small but handsomely finished office room of the big pier building which towered above cobblestoned Twelfth Avenue and the newly-built express highway which flowed north along the western edge of Manhattan, Inspector Thomas Gregg, chief of the Bureau of Detectives, spoke to seven elderly men.

"Without disrespect to you, gentlemen," he said gruffly, "I must say this sounds juvenile and screwy to me. The idea of a super-criminal staging a come-back after twenty years is ridiculous on the face of it. And there were no super-criminals twenty years ago. Why, I had one devil of a time even getting reports from the mid-west on this-er-Albert Millett. And look at the picture I got from Arizona —a smooth-faced kid with buck teeth. It's so faded you can scarcely decipher it."

"Inspector Gregg, you are making a grave mistake in taking this matter so lightly," said Carl Fenwick, the theatrical producer, in a solemn voice. "We were all young then, some younger than others, and photography was bad. You didn't know Al Millett. We did."

A sort of psychic shiver seemed to ripple around the group of seven at his words. Even Inspector Gregg felt it, and the hackles wanted to rise on his thick, red neck. This made the chief detective mad. He fairly scowled around the group which half-encircled him.

Seven elderly, influential, wealthy, distinguished men. He told them off mentally. Now that he thought of it, this was the first time Gregg had ever been in close contact with any of these prominent men-the very first time he had even heard of them appearing publicly together.

Clyde Dickson, gaunt-faced, with dark and brooding eyes, an unusually thick shock of grey hair on his oddly pointed head, was huddled deep in a leather armchair. He was the owner of the highly successful Palladium Club-one of New York's most luxurious night spots.

Stocky, broad of beam, heavy-jowled, but visibly short of legs despite their massiveness, Bernard J. Andrews leaned on a beautifully carved cane as rugged as himself as he stood there. Andrews was the president of a nationally known radio station.

Paul Corbin, owner and operator of a small chain of exclusive night clubs and cocktail bars, stood next. Corbin was small, slender, with an effeminate sort of face out of which looked large, tragic eyes which, in themselves, were beautiful. He wore loosely tailored tweeds which almost looked too bulky, too mannish for him.

John Gifford, massive-chested and craggy of features, with arms that were a trifle abnormal in length, sat beside Dickson and spoke to him in deep whispers. Gifford was a well-known operator of a huge amusement park at Coney Island and the designer of the breath-taking Leap-for-Life rocket ride.

Gordon Drake, a well known figure in the motion picture industry, stood looking out the window. Drake was the most handsomely proportioned man present. At fifty, his body was still classical in its lines. But he marred the sweep of his fine figure by wearing a light opera cape about his shoulders. And he always wore gloves.

Kenneth Meade, a renowned restaurateur, gaunt of feature and spare of frame, attired in evening clothes for his appearance at Milady's Salon, his newest and finest restaurant, was tapping on the desk and frowning anxiously.

Fenwick, the seventh man, was a tall, cadaverous individual clad in severe black and wearing a high, stiff collar which gave him a clerical air. Had he been funny instead of lugubrious, he could have walked right out on the stage in any one of his productions as the stage parson.

All of these men were prominent and respected. There was nothing particularly odd about them individually. But, together, they exerted a queer effect upon the inspector that was almost weird. It was an intangible feeling. Perhaps it was due to the fact that these men were noted for living so utterly alone. None of them were married. Their private lives were simple, retiring, exclusive. No two of them lived together, except the Marcy brothers, who had not arrived for this meeting.

Baffled, the inspector shook his head and scowled.

"All right, all right," he said. "Let's go over it again. This Al Millett was guilty of several minor crimes some twenty-odd years ago. The worst we can find is that train robbery in Utah, and he served a sentence for that. He called himself 'The Fang,' theatrically leaving a tiger tooth as a marker on the scenes of his depredations.

"The penitentiary sentence must have taken the starch out of him. He abandoned crime upon his release to become a showman. He joined Crowley and Buckill, the then-famous circus. That was the hey-day of circus business. They puffed him up as the 'Fang,' the man with the terrible and bloody history and the criminal mind which, if loosed, could wreck the country. And all he did was ride wild horses, shoot blank pistols, and generally exhibit himself as the madman from the gory West.

"That, gentlemen, may have gone over big in those days, but no hick town in the whole United States would give that sort of side-show attraction a second glance today.

"And, as for this Al Millett, the police of this day and time have never even heard of him. I am positive that you are needlessly alarmed over this twenty-year-old bugaboo —"

"But you don't understand!" broke in Gordon Drake, whirling about at the window. "We've explained that Millett disappeared suddenly just twenty years ago-right after his wife died. He blamed us for her death because we wouldn't back him in a venture of his own. He disappeared utterly, after swearing vengeance on us, individually and collectively. And, once a year, on the anniversary of his wife's death-for the past three years-he's been sending us grotesque warnings of hate and disaster. We showed them to you. They came from different parts of the world."

"We tried to trace these messages, but we couldn't," John Gifford spoke in his deep voice. "We thought at first like you are thinking now, but time has changed us. And this time we received this message which promises death to us, one at a time. We would have been foolish not to come to the police for aid."

Inspector Gregg picked up one of the seven copies of identical messages from "The Fang," and read it again.

In block-printed letters of red on black parchment paper, the words stared up at him.

MY TIME FOR REVENGE DRAWS NEAR AT LAST ON THIS TWENTIETH ANNIVERSARY OF BURNOOSE'S DEATH. WHEN THE *CHARLEMAGNE* DOCKS IN NEW YORK NEXT TRIP YOU SHALL FEEL THE FANG OF DOOM. ONE BY ONE NINE MEN SHALL DIE-IF I MAY CALL YOU MEN. WHO SHALL GO FIRST? I INVITE YUH TO MY DEBARKATION.

Inspector Gregg cleared his throat and glanced swiftly around the circle. He was surprised to find all seven men watching him in nervous intensity.

"This is theatrical hokum," he snorted. "It stinks of melodrama. I'm amazed that you let such a crank letter disturb you. And whoever heard of murder by appointment?"

"Inspector Gregg," said Carl Fenwick in a sepulchral voice, "please bear in mind that this Al Millett was a far more desperate and depraved character than you are giving him credit for, and that he hates the nine of us with a vindictiveness that fairly seethes in its intensity."

"It's too bad the Marcy brothers aren't here to talk to you, Inspector Gregg," added Paul Corbin in his queer, husky voice. "They knew Millett more intimately, and can give you fuller details."

"Anyway, we've increased the police guard for the *Charlemagne's* docking, and I have a cordon of plainclothes men on hand to apprehend this Millett guy for questioning and investigation. And you are here to point him out to us. So we'll pull his 'fangs' before he can even sink 'em in a piece of pie at the Automat."

"If we point him out," observed Kenneth Meade in his stilted, slow, hoarse manner of speech. "He may be in hiding—a stowaway. Perhaps he's changed his appearance-other men have. He was fiendishly clever with disguise. I wish—"

"The Marcy brothers!" ejaculated Gordon Drake from the window. "I see their car just pulling up. They're not getting out, of course."

"Why should they?" commented John Gifford quickly. "The boat's docking. We'd better get out of here ourselves."

"We'll see what the Marcys say, first," decided Inspector Gregg, leading the way swiftly out to the parking lanes, the others following him more slowly.

The Marcy car, resplendent with glittering nickel and liveried chauffeur, was parked in a little cleared space back from the front lines, as if shrinking from publicity.

In the rear seat, two brothers with faces startlingly similar, save that Benjamin wore a mustache, while Lyle was clean-shaven, looked out at the approaching detective. Famous as theatre owners, they shrank from notoriety.

"Well?" Benjamin Marcy's mustache bristled at the converging group, although his piercing eyes had the same brooding, world-weary, yet anxious look that all these worried men seemed to have. "You don't expect us to get out and jam into that crowd, do you? I'm tired."

"Just tell me in few words what you can about this guy Millett," Gregg spoke swiftly.

As one, the two brothers leaned forward.

"Al Millett must be a madman," Lyle Marcy stated, his lean face darkening. "We were all in the show business together many years ago.

"Millett got terribly angry when we wouldn't pool our money and back him in a crazy wild-west show of his own. His wife died, and he disappeared, after threatening us with revenge. As for his coming back now—"

"We don't believe it!" Benjamin Marcy broke in fiercely. "This whole thing is somebody's idea of a bad joke."

"Whose?" demanded Andrews, panting from his laborious exertions to arrive at the car in a group with the others, leaning heavily on his cane.

"You Marcys know you're as worried about this thing as any of the rest of us."

"The only thing I'm worried about is the publicity," denied Benjamin Marcy savagely. "Lyle and I hate publicity!"

The sound of a hoarse, bass siren shook the air around them. Growing commotion at the docks warned them.

"Come on, you men, and take your positions on the second level," cried Gregg. "All passengers disembark there. You can't miss your man, if he comes ashore."

Leaving the grimly waiting Marcy brothers, the group made its way to the spacious second level where alphabetical partitions awaited tourists and luggage.

Pulleys creaked, winches groaned, and the huge liner came gently to rest. In a moment the gangways came sliding down, and people were pouring along them like ants. A pair of plain-clothes officers stood by at each exit, watching for the chief inspector's signal. Gregg watched the faces of his companions who went to their appointed stations, staring nervously all along the side of the great ship and up and down the gangways.

Nothing happened. The stream of passengers dwindled, died away. And no alarm had been given.

"Well, gentlemen," grunted Inspector Gregg a bit peevishly an hour later. "After all your hullabaloo, your Nemesis doesn't seem to have even got off the boat. If you can wait another hour, I'll have the ship inspected from stem to stern to make sure your man is not aboard."

"Please," whispered Meade in his odd articulation. "We must be certain."

"Where's Andrews?" demanded Drake suddenly. "He's supposed to be watching the D to G section."

"There he is," Gregg pointed. "Guess he just went down to the washroom for a moment. You haven't seen this building until you tour it. It is conveniently arranged so that everything is accessible from almost any part of building or grounds. Well-engineered construction. Well, let's go on board and —"

The sudden wail of a police ambulance beat upon their eardrums and rose in a sharp crescendo of sound. Police whistles shrilled. Somewhere a woman screamed. A uniformed officer dashed up to Inspector Gregg and began murmuring in his ear. At once Gregg stiffened. He motioned brusquely for the policeman to lead the way. As they followed, very white of face, the seven elderly men who had been responsible for him being here tonight fell in line as he passed their posts, and streamed along after him.

Down in the parking area the night had turned into bedlam. Red-faced patrolmen were forming lines to keep back the surging crowd and divert traffic. Screaming sirens announced the arrival of radio and squad cars. Frantic terror clutched at the hearts of the men following the chief detective as they realized the direction they were heading.

The Marcy limousine, still in an area of shadows, but no longer avoiding publicity, was before them. The car itself was harshly outlined now in the concentrated glare of police hand torches. The first thing of significance that caught Inspector Gregg's eye was the liveried chauffeur, lolling over his wheel. The back of his skull was a bloody ruin, bashed in by some blunt instrument.

The inspector's eyes went to the rear of the car. He braced himself for this look. The uniformed man had told him what he would find. Even so, hardened to crime as he was, he recoiled. His usually placid face went grey, eyes widening in a shock of horror and revulsion.

Benjamin and Lyle Marcy were still together in the back seat, but they had slumped down. Where their abdomens should have been, there was a gaping hole in each corpse, in the back of which the very spinal columns were exposed. Blood and viscera splattered and fouled the seat, the sides, and the floor of the tonneau.

The faces of the two brothers were frozen in grimaces of agonized horror. Their sightless, staring eyes seemed still to be looking at the hideous, brutal death monster that had struck them down. A very bad joke, indeed, Messrs. Marcy!

Paul Corbin had pushed forward behind the chief detective. He saw, and a shrill, high-pitched scream left his lips.

"God!" he shrieked. "The Fang! He's killed the Marcys. We told you, Inspector Gregg-but you wouldn't believe —"

"Get a grip on yourself, man!" snapped Gregg curtly. "We'll see about this. There's been murder, yes; but shut up about this Fang business if you don't want publicity. You're as jittery as a woman."

He turned to the police captain near at hand. "Okay, Donaldson, boil it down for me-quick!"

"Very little, inspector," was the grimly terse answer. "No sound, nobody seen approaching or leaving the car because all eyes were on the docking *Charlemagne*. A late-arriving taxi driver noticed the slumped body of the chauffeur, took one look, and yelled for help. We are holding him for questioning. Rather weird, sir."

"Check," nodded Gregg. "I'll say it's weird. No clues?"

"Only this, sir," said the captain, and he held out a large saber tooth —a tiger fang. "I found this in the front seat by the chauffeur."

As he stared, Gregg's color drained out of his cheeks. Was it possible, after all, that Al Millett had come back after a lapse of twenty years to avenge himself for a fancied wrong?

His eyes went to the big, lighted liner with her rakishly slanted funnels still smoking at her berth. His men had watched every egress from that vessel. Seven anxious and determined men had gazed carefully at each disembarking passenger. After forewarning his victims, had some fantastic, theatrically inclined madman eluded all detection and slipped ashore to commit his first murder?

"All right, Donaldson," Gregg spoke. "You're in charge. Get pics, prints, suspects-everything you can. I'll go over it with you later. As for you seven gentlemen, I think, perhaps, you'd better go —"

A cop from a prowl car dashed up.

"Inspector," he saluted hurriedly, "there's been a near-riot at the Marcy Gold Slipper. Monk Gorman at the head of a big mob pulled a hijack stunt right under the noses of the theater crowds. Captain Waltham is over there hollering for you."

Marcy Gold Slipper! The finest, newest playhouse the Marcy brothers had built. And Monk Gorman-Monk Gorman, a muscle-man of no outstanding intelligence-had headed a successful robbery there! Robbery at their own theater while the Marcys themselves got murdered here! It didn't make sense, didn't tie in with the story of the nine alarmed men at all.

"On second thought," Gregg said to the white-lipped and shivering men behind him-towering figures in the entertainment world, but frightened children beside him now —"you men had better go home and stay there until you hear from me again. As soon as I look into both of these crimes closely, I'll get in touch with each of you. I'll furnish a police escort to see you home, a guard to stay all night, if you wish."

Paul Corbin, the excitable, laughed hysterically. He was assisted away by two uniformed officers. His wild cry came back over his shoulder.

"We'll need the whole police force to guard us now, Inspector Gregg," he shouted sobbingly. "For whoever heard of murder by appointment?"

Chapter III
Enter the Phantom

The towering, midtown *Clarion* Building, which housed the city's leading newspaper reared high in the night mists. Its windows glowed with lights; from its lower floors came the pounding of rotary presses-giving evidence that here activity went on perpetually, day and night.

It was well after midnight when a large but unobtrusive Cadillac sedan swung around the corner, its lights dim. It slowed near the chrome and glass doors which were the imposing front entrance of the *Clarion* Building.

Four slouch-hatted men peered from the open front and rear windows of the sedan. Their hat brims, snapped low, obscured their hard, brutal faces.

"Stop right here, Tony." A broken-nosed man leaned forward from the rear to tap a pallid, nervous driver.

"Okay, Gus!" Tony applied the brakes, but even when he had the car stopped at the curb, he kept the engine purring. "Hope this ain't gonna take long —"

"Don't be so jittery! This is a cinch!" Gus was leaning from the window, eyes covering the pavement. Every time a pedestrian neared the front doors of the building, especially when some hurrying newsman or other person connected with the paper entered those doors, Gus tensed a little, hand darting to his armpit holster. "Be ready, guys-we gotta pull this job smooth!"

"Say, who we gonna smoke?" the hatchet-faced man next to Gus demanded now. "This is the *Clarion's* joint, ain't it? Seems to me I heard somethin' special about this place —"

"You sure did, Choppy!" the fourth man, in the front, spoke through a gash of a mouth from which a cigarette dangled to bob with his words. "Hell, the *Clarion's* the rag that acts the contact for that bird called *the Phantom!*"

A strange awed dread followed the pronunciation of that sobriquet —a dread which seemed instantly to course through his companions, like a wave. Hate, the hate born of utter fear, gleamed from their eyes.

The Phantom! Throughout the underworld of the entire nation, that name had become a byword of fear. The Phantom, lone Nemesis of Crime, a living, elusive scourge who personified the antidote to crime!

"The Phantom!" Tony cried, hoarsely now. "Say, Gus-is *that* who we're waitin' for?"

Gus quickly shook his head. "Take it easy, guys! The Big Shot ain't interested in anyone unless he sticks his nose into this-which he won't if he's got brains! They say the Phantom made things pretty tough for us, sendin' so many of us up the river-but this boss is one guy he can't buck! Naw, we ain't after that slippery bird. We're just doin' a job on a punk named Eddie Collins, who draws them funnies you see in the papers."

"Funnies? You mean comic cartoons?" the gash-mouthed man said in surprise. "Hell, what do we want to bump a guy who draws *them* for?"

"Maybe the Big Shot don't like his funny pitchers, Pete," Tony put in, with sardonic mirth.

"You don't know how right you are!" Gus chortled, a purposeful look in his eyes. "But you just follow my lead —I'm runnin' this job. 'Course I'd rather be with Monk and the rest-they got another big heist job. The boss certainly knows how to get things movin' fast-why, he's only taken over the mobs last night, and we've done more than we did in years for our old big shots! The coppers'll never keep up with us now! Hell, there was hundreds of 'em down at that pier when the boat landed, and right under their noses —" he paused, as if realizing he was getting loquacious.

But the others broke in eagerly now. "You was there, Gus. Did you see him?"

The broken-nosed Gus swelled instinctively with a sense of importance. "Sure," his voice was unconvincingly casual. "Sure I seen him."

"What'd he look like, Gus? What kinda guy was he?"

"Well now-he was kinda muffled up in a coat. Couldn't spot his mug. But I seen his work-and that was enough! What he done to them two brothers, all by himself —" Despite himself he gave a shudder. "Don't know how the hell he done it. I'd sure hate to be on the wrong side o' that guy, and —"

Abruptly he broke off, body tensing, hand snaking from his armpit holster. A taxi had just pulled to the curb, ahead of the parked sedan. Out of it leaped a figure, turning in the gloom as the cab rolled on its way.

The figure strode down the pavement towards the *Clarion* entrance. Light from a street-lamp revealed him in the next instant. A stocky young man, hardly more than a grown kid-he was walking hurriedly, carrying a flat envelope under one arm.

"It's the Collins guy all right!" Gus spoke quick, low. "Okay, Tony! Step up that motor-he's comin' by! Me an' Pete'll use the rods."

Oblivious, the youth on the pavement walked on-coming diagonally abreast of the sedan in the next instant as two automatics trained their beads directly on his hurrying figure.

"Okay, Tony!"

The purring motor of the Cadillac rose abruptly to a vibrating clamor as Tony's foot jammed down the accelerator. The two guns leveled from the front and rear windows. Flame leaped livid in the night from their jerking muzzles!

The motor almost drowned completely the quick reports, so they were not heard by any passing motorists.

The four shots flamed in swift succession.

As if grabbed by some unseen giant hand in the dark, the youth on the pavement stopped in his tracks. His stocky frame whirled completely around. His hands clutched at his chest-and through his clawing fingers blood spurted darkly.

Slowly, his knees buckled. He dropped on them. In contrast to the darkness, his face showed white, agonized as it turned towards the roaring but immobile sedan.

Then a choking cry as of defiance came from the youngster. He still clutched the manila envelope-and some miracle of purpose seemed to spur his riddled body into motion again. Crablike, half-crawling in the gloom, he was moving forward.

The broken-nosed Gus saw that movement, gave vent to a livid oath. He yanked the rear door of the Cadillac open, his eyes peering up and down the street. It was dark, deserted. He leaped out, gun in hand. Pete and hatchet-faced Choppy followed.

Simultaneously the riddled youth, evidently seeing them coming, was suddenly, miraculously on wabbly legs-running, darting like a wild, wounded animal, instinctively trying to lose himself from his hunters.

Clutching the envelope he actually reached the corner, rounding the building as the others gained in their pursuit. They did not fire now-for their quarry was only a vague blur in the almost opaque gloom caused by the shadowy side of the building, near a railed areaway.

In that gloom, Gus, Pete, and Choppy closed in. Their hands groped. There was the sound of a scuffle-the ripping of paper-confusion.

The three gangsters became accustomed enough to the dark to regain vision. They found themselves in a tangle.

Gus cursed. "He went over the rail! He can't get far with them slugs in him-an' I don't know if we got all we want! Come on, guys, we gotta find him!"

They climbed over the rail, dropping into the lower areaway. Groping in the gloom, guns still in hand.

And at that same instant, Eddie Collins, youthful cartoonist, was swaying against the cage of a freight elevator which was speeding upwards inside the building. He heard his own blood dripping to the floor of the ascending lift. Torpor was dragging at his agonized body. Yet, like some stubborn spark, a fierce determination was keeping him alive and active.

Floors went by in a blur, painfully slow. Up through the building the elevator ascended. Then it stopped of its own accord, on the top floor, up in the tower.

Collins pulled his coat about his chest as if hoping to stem the flow of his own blood. He groaned with the effort of opening the gate, staggered out through a corridor, thence through swing service doors.

Somehow he found the frosted-glass doors he sought. He pushed into a lighted, well-appointed anteroom. He pushed on through, reached another door, marked private.

Eddie Collins grabbed the door handle-burst into the huge, private office whose French windows looked high over the Manhattan night.

At his rude entry, two men jerked up startled, surprised heads.

Frank Havens, elderly, rugged-faced owner of the *Clarion* and a string of other equally powerful papers throughout the nation, rose to his feet from the big desk where he had been sitting, proof-sheets bearing gruesome murder-news before him.

Richard Curtis Van Loan, wealthy young idler and man-about-town, who was here as Mr. Havens's friend and guest, lifted his bored, world-wearied grey eyes in questioning annoyance. Seated in a comfortable chair, Van Loan was puffing idly at a cigarette, his immaculately dress-trousered legs crossed.

Then, before anyone could speak, the bored Richard Curtis Van Loan suddenly leaped from his chair. His grey eyes lost their ennui, became sharp slits. It was he who saw the oozing, crimson trickle coming from beneath Collins's coat and dripping soundlessly to the soft carpet.

Collins's body swayed giddily as Van Loan leaped forward. The latter's strong arms reached out, caught the young cartoonist even as the youth went limp, collapsing.

"This man's been shot!" Van Loan said, his customary drawl sharp now.

Havens's momentary annoyance turned to quick alarm. The publisher grabbed an inter-office phone, called a downstairs office secretary, ordering that a doctor be summoned. Then he went over to where Van Loan had carried the riddled youth to a lounge and placed him on it.

"Collins!" he cried, all concern now. "What happened? Who —?"

The eyes of Eddie Collins, already going dull, flickered. His lips moved. A sighing rattle made the words which came from his throat difficult to hear.

"Envelope —" he gasped. "Envelope! Gangsters-probably still down in areaway cellar looking for me. Freight elevator-They got it-from me-but they aren't sure —"

"Got what, Collins? What do you mean?" Havens spoke with fierce bafflement. "How could you —a comic strip man-be mixed up with thugs, with shooting!"

"Envelope tells," Collins repeated. "Big case-Mr. Havens. I was doing it for a feature-when murder story broke. Bringing it for-the Phantom-now."

Even in his agony, he pronounced that name with reverent awe.

Havens stiffened. The publisher's eyes flashed to his worldly young friend, Richard Curtis Van Loan. And he got a fresh shock of surprise.

For Van Loan had suddenly gone into a whirl of swift action! He had peeled off his dress coat. In his hands was a flat leather kit, which was snapped open, to reveal a mirror and an array of tubes and jars.

Again Collins's gasping voice interrupted. "Case-for Phantom! God, if only you could-get him now, Mr. Havens." He sobbed. "Envelope-thugs got it —"

Havens administered to the riddled man as best he could while Van Loan worked away on his queer little kit.

When the publisher turned toward Van Loan, his jaw gaped.

Van, standing close, eyes darting from the man on the lounge to his own mirror, was still dabbing his face with a special charcoal. In seconds his handsome, world-weary features had almost completely vanished! In their place had grown another visage-the face of Eddie Collins!

It was not a semblance that could stand close inspection under bright light, being more an impressionistic sort of job, the likeness cleverly created by a few lines, by shading. Nor did Van Loan take any more precious time adding to it.

"Give me Collins's coat, Frank-quickly! It ought to be enough!"

Van Loan pulled on the coat and assumed a stoop. Though he was tall, he seemed by his posture to look even more like the bullet-riddled cartoonist.

So swiftly had he made the transformation that now, before the dying Collins saw what was happening, his own "double" was darting out of the office in a swift blur of motion which concealed both the incongruity of his dress, and his makeshift disguise.

Collins hadn't seen any of this. Nor had Collins dreamed that Richard Curtis Van Loan, the rich playboy he had seen so many times, was actually the mysterious and amazing sleuth whose fearsome name he had breathed, whose services he had demanded —*the Phantom Detective* whose perilous exploits in the dark byways of the underworld were known by the police the world over.

Only Frank Havens knew that Van Loan was the Phantom; only Havens knew how this seemingly bored young millionaire really gave his energies and lifeblood to the most exacting and dangerous task on earth-the tracking down of baffling and ruthless criminals.

Even to Havens, the Phantom was always a source of surprise and wonder. His quick-working brain was too fast to follow: his quick changes in disguise left the publisher gasping-as they had left him now.

Yet Van had acted with logic while acting with speed. Snatches of barely coherent speech from Eddie Collins had registered themselves indelibly on his mind: Freight elevator-thugs-still looking for Collins —

The Phantom scarcely knew Collins, only vaguely remembered seeing the youthful cartoonist around the *Clarion* Building. Certainly he had no idea what this was all about. As a matter of fact, his mind had been on other matters-on a bizarre, double murder which Frank Havens had called him down to discuss. But when Collins had come in, riddled-bringing crime flagrantly to this very building-Van had promptly dropped all other thoughts.

The Phantom reached the freight elevator, with its blood-stained floor, in the next instant. His lithe body pushed into the car-his long arm slammed the gate shut and started the elevator down. He reached into his pocket, into which he had transferred a fully loaded blue-steel Colt .45 automatic, U.S. Army, M-1911 —the favorite weapon of the Phantom.

Musty odors of the cellar rose to engulf the slow-descending cage. The Phantom tensed, adopting again the pose of Eddie Collins. His hand was on his gun, his thumb snapping back the safety catch. He knew he was deliberately playing with Death in his risky scheme.

The cellar loomed, dim and empty. Nobody in here. He hurried across it on soft-soled feet, eyes alert. Reaching the door of the areaway, he opened it softly. Night breeze, still carrying the heat of the Indian summer, met him.

He was out in the areaway like a drifting shadow. In the gloom his keen eyes, which had the cat-like gift of piercing darkness, glanced about. No one here. A surge of disappointment, a sense of anticlimax, narrowed his eyes. Despite his swiftness, had he been too long in coming?

He vaulted over the rail then, to the street. Cautiously, again emulating Collins-even staggering a little now-he moved down the block. The nearest street-lamp flecked his face. He caught a blur of movement and he dropped to the pavement like a deflating sack. Dropped as his every nerve combined in sixth sense to flash the warning to his alert brain!

Two guns flamed livid out of the dark, their reports shattering the quiet side street off Broadway. Bullets whined over the prone Phantom as he hugged the sidewalk. They ricocheted inches away, chipping the paving.

"Got him this time, Gus?"

"Better make sure!"

Van rolled as he heard the coarse voices. He saw three slouch-hatted figures charging from another dark doorway of the building, where they had been prowling.

His Colt snaked out. Eyes grim, he fired even as he rolled into position —a blind, snap shot at the charging trio.

One of the three, a gash-mouthed man, recoiled with a scream of pain. His hand clawed at his shoulder, blood spurting through the wound.

The other two also recoiled, amazed by the counter-attack. The broken-nosed man in their lead stared at the Phantom, who even now was leaping to his feet.

Madly he fired his automatic-fired as a suddenly panic-stricken man would fire.

Van ducked sideways, out of the lamp-light. The bullets went so far wide he didn't hear them. Not only was the man's apparent confusion spoiling his aim-in his left hand he was busily clutching a manila envelope! The Phantom grimly raised his Colt again. He drew a careful bead on the man with the envelope.

"Beat it, guys!" the third man was yelling. "The shootin's been heard-The cops're comin'!"

Crack!

It was Van's Colt that blazed in that split-second.

A hoarse cry burst from the broken-nosed thug. As if it suddenly burned him, he dropped the envelope. It fluttered to the pavement. The Phantom's well-aimed shot had creased his wrist-making his pained muscles release their grip.

Across Broadway now two bluecoats came into view —a traffic and a beat cop, blowing their whistles, reaching with free hands for guns. The scream of a prowl-car added to the clamor.

Van hurled forward. The broken-nosed thug, nursing his wrist with his mouth, hesitated. Then, leaving the envelope, dashed on around the corner.

The Phantom scooped the envelope up without stopping in his pace. Rounding the corner, he saw the trio piling into a dark Cadillac sedan which started rolling from the curb in the next split-second, gears grinding raucously. Van leaped after it, then ducked.

Glass in the rear window shattered as a gun smashed its muzzle through. A fusillade of lead came from the departing car as it careened around the next block, swiftly disappearing. An oncoming green prowl-car sped in pursuit.

The Phantom, already grimly certain the gang car had had enough of a start to make a safe getaway, whirled back toward the *Clarion* Building, envelope in hand. He moved so swiftly that the police did not see him.

Again he used the freight elevator, riding back to the tower. The Phantom had struck again and disappeared.

Chapter IV
Gargoyle Clue

Van Loan entered the private office. He saw Frank Havens standing, eyes filled with deep pain. A grave-faced man he recognized as the *Clarion's* doctor was turning away from the lounge where Eddie Collins lay very still, a glassy look in his eyes.

The doctor shook his head. Then started as he saw the dead man's double in the doorway.

"Don't be alarmed, Doctor," said Van in Collins's voice. "The Phantom-not a ghost. Will you leave us, please?"

The physician left and Van quickly shut the door. He glanced at Collins. "Too bad, Frank-he seemed a plucky kid," his voice came hushed.

Havens spoke huskily. "I can't understand it, Van! Collins was just a comic strip man, a hard ambitious worker. Why he should be murdered like this —" He broke off then, with new concern. "But you, Van! What have you been doing? Did you see his murderers?"

"I did, and drew a little blood," Van returned grimly, as he substituted Collins's coat for his own. His long arm scooped up Havens's phone. Matter-of-factly, he put in a call to the police. "My deception worked for a moment. The gangsters were lurking, thinking Collins was hidden somewhere down there. The police are after them now. I guess they'll be coming up here any minute. Before they come, let's see what we can make of this envelope."

Quickly he took it to Havens's desk. Its flap was loose. Evidently hands had already been rummaging in it. For a moment the Phantom thought, with a pang of disappointment, that it was empty. Then he drew out its only contents —a single torn piece of white paper. Black pen-sketching and lettering showed on it.

"Seems to be some sort of cartooning!" Van observed. "Collins's work, apparently."

He spread it on the desk, and Havens came over to peer at it with him. The first thing that met their eyes was a bizarre ink-sketch. It showed a skull, a lurid death's head, and beneath it a playing card —a joker.

Letters printed underneath read: *"Impossible but true is the Gargoyle Club, which sometimes meets secretly at —"*

Here the paper was torn, the rest of the sentence missing.

"Gargoyle Club?" Havens read aloud. "What can *that* be? And that joker and skull?"

The publisher broke off, the blood suddenly draining from his face. For now his eyes had fallen on three other ink sketches which comprised the remainder of the torn cartoon.

One of the three was torn, not clearly distinguishable. But the other two were full and clear. Two faces, both similar, save that one bristled with a mustache while the other was clean-shaven, stared up at them.

With one accord the eyes of Havens and Van Loan went from that cartoon to the wet front-page proof-sheet on Havens's desk.

There, in a photograph this time, those two same faces stared out of the front page, beneath the bold black headline:

TWO SHOWMEN BRUTALLY MURDERED

"Good grief!" Havens gasped, his face white now. "The Marcy brothers! Collins drew them here! That's the sensational case I was trying to persuade you to tackle, Van! The case involving all those big men of the amusement world-the nine who told the police of this criminal, Al Millett, the Fang-who apparently came to America on the *Charlemagne* tonight-last night. It's nearly morning."

Van's eyes narrowed to slits. His keen mind had absorbed the facts of the strange case. The shake-up of four mobs preceding the landing of the ship-the newly organized mob of four dead leaders suddenly cutting loose-the police baffled by a terrific outbreak of crime and violence. And now-this!

"It seems this case had landed on us personally, Frank," he said grimly. "It's reached out and hit the *Clarion*! But look here. The murder was just a few hours ago, correct? And until now these men involved had not come forward into the limelight."

"That's right! And for some reason, Collins drew a picture-maybe he hoped it would break into the news section —"

"That's the point, Frank," Van said slowly. "Collins did *not* just draw this picture. Or even last night! The ink on it indicates clearly that it's at least a week or so old!"

"But, Van!" Havens protested. "That means Collins must have known something of the Marcys before anyone dreamed —"

"Precisely. Can you suggest any way he might have worked on such a tack?"

"I can't even hazard a guess, Van. Collins stuck to his cartooning in the comic strip. True, I remember his saying something about changing his line-but as for this drawing, with its skull and joker, and that stuff about the Gargoyle Club —" Confused, his grim eyes went to the lounge-as if bitterly wishing for the death-sealed lips of Eddie Collins to speak the secret that they could never now reveal.

Van, meanwhile, looked at the third and torn face on the cartoon. Only the top of the head and the eyes showed.

"Look here, Frank. Something queer about this picture."

Havens, looking, noticed a blackish protrusion on top of the head, as though the cartoonist's pen had slipped. "An ink-blot probably," he said. "Makes it look as if something is sticking in the head there. Funny —"

He broke off, stiffening, as heavy feet sounded at the office door. Van Loan swiftly took a black silk domino from his pocket and slipped it on over his Collins make-up.

A bluecoat, followed by two men in plainclothes, entered. One of the latter spoke, eyes instantly going with recognition to the publisher.

"There's been some shooting in the street, Mr. Havens. Was that why you called Police Head —"

He stopped short as his eyes glimpsed the prone, inert body of Collins. That was his first surprise. His second came as he and the other two policemen saw the domino-masked Phantom, who now stepped forward, eyes gleaming through his mask-holes.

"It's all right, gentlemen. I called. I'm the Phantom-already on the case." As he spoke his palm flipped open.

The two detectives and the bluecoat stared in awe at the scintillating sparkle which was revealed. A sparkle of matchless diamond chips, forming the design of a domino mask against a badge of platinum.

The emblem of the Phantom! An emblem which every law-enforcement agent throughout the nation had been taught to respect.

Van gave crisp commands. "You can take over here. Conduct the usual investigation. Call Homicide and the Medical Examiner. This man is Edward Collins, who worked for Mr. Havens and —"

The shrill buzz of the inter-office telephone interrupted. Havens quickly snapped the key, picking up the instrument. "Hello-yes?" He turned. "Is one of you men Lieutenant Donovan? Patrolman downstairs is asking for you."

The larger of the two detectives grabbed the instrument with a gruff, "Thanks."

"Yes?" he said. "What's that? Okay-be right down!"

He whirled from the phone, his face beefy with excitement. "Radio flash! Signal 30! There's a stick-up at the Palladium Club!"

Van tensed even as Havens looked momentarily bewildered. In his social life, as a night-club habitue, he knew about the Palladium, the most popular of hot-spots. But his keen retentive mind was telling him something else.

"That's Clyde Dickson's club, Frank!" he crisped. "Dickson-one of the nine men involved in this case!"

He whirled on the detectives. "You two men stay here! Officer, you come with us. Is there a cruiser downstairs?"

The detectives nodded.

"All right, Mr. Havens and I will use it!"

It was the regular express elevator which took the Phantom, Havens, and the bluecoat down to the street level. Hurriedly they ran out to the curb. Two prowl-cars were pulling away, sirens screaming. The cruiser, a small sedan, stood purring, a police driver impatiently shifting at its wheel, the radio blaring repeatedly: "Signal 30! All cars in Division 1 —"

The bluecoat with Van explained. And it was unnecessary for the Phantom again to display his badge. An instant later, with Van and Havens in the rear, the cruiser sped screaming through the night, headed up Broadway.

As it approached the fifties, the scream of other sirens became audible ahead. The cruiser tore around Fifty-Second Street-agleam at this late hour with its line of nightclubs, all going full tilt.

The cruiser squealed on its tires, as it came before the vast neon sign: "Palladium Club." Prowl-cars here were banked two deep-but some were speeding off, hell-bent. From within the club came sounds of pandemonium.

"Better stay here awhile, Frank!" Van crisped, as he leaped from the cruiser.

The Phantom, together with police who were still rushing into the club, hurried through its palatial entrance.

Many times, as Richard Van Loan, bored socialite, he had gone into this lavish club. He knew its interior well. Yet as he rushed in now, he scarcely recognized it.

The well-appointed hall of the club looked as if a cyclone had struck it. Though wall lights illumined the place, the huge chandelier which had furnished the main light was shattered where it hung.

On the dance floor, tables and chairs were overturned. The band dais was a confusion of tumbled instruments, overturned music stands. Above, swinging crazily and incongruously, was a brilliant-studded but empty trapeze on ropes.

Van identified it at once; he remembered that the main attraction of this club was an aerial artiste —a young girl known only as "Queen Stella" who furnished a new thrill to jaded society crowds with her acrobatics.

All this Van's eyes took in with a swift comprehensive glance. Then his gaze went across the floor. He saw a huddling, terrified mass of people. Women in low-cut gowns; men in faultless dress suits. All jabbering with that hysterical excitement that comes after a crisis.

"My jewels-they took my jewels!" he heard a woman shrieking.

"They got away with my wallet, damn them!" a man cursed.

Police were listening sympathetically. Other police were scurrying about the floor, taking command of the exclusive club. Some Van saw at exit doors, shaking their heads.

The Phantom realized, even as Frank Havens now came up behind him, that he had come just after the end of the stick-up. The mobsters had obviously cleared out.

"Since we are here, let's look around," said the Phantom. "Where is Dickson?"

No one had seen the club owner since the excitement began.

Frank Havens saw the Phantom hurl suddenly forward-running toward Dickson's office.

Van's dash carried him to a rear door, so well shadowed behind drapes that as yet the police had not noticed it.

The door was closed. But as the Phantom neared it, sounds behind it grew louder. And then not only Van, but several nearby policemen, stiffened-eyes going wide.

From behind the closed door came a sudden, hoarse scream! A scream which rose, in blood-curdling agony and terror!

"You!" the scream came. "It's you! No!" Shrill now it rose, in a high, quavering pitch. "Don't —Oh, God —*don't* —"

Even as the Phantom yanked at the locked door, that agonized cry broke off with horrible abruptness. There was a ghastly thud —a shatter as of glass.

Eyes slitted in their mask-holes, the Phantom whirled to the men behind him. "Give me a hand!" he crisped. "Get this door open!"

Chapter V
The Fang Strikes Again

Brawny bluecoats promptly charged that door. Wood splintered with the successive impacts of their big shoulders. The door burst from its lock. The Phantom, gun whipping out, was the first to leap into the room, police following at his heels.

In one swift comprehensive glance, Van's eyes took in the scene. Three sights stood out at once. A safe, its door open and still swinging, its interior bare and gaping; a broken window, looking out into black gloom; and-on the floor —a prone heap, lying terribly still.

The Phantom rushed to the broken window. Outside was an alleyway, but it led to a high, dead-end wall. His keen eyes told him that no one was there, although as he backed away, policemen climbed through the window with flashlights and guns to investigate.

Van darted back through the room. He found two more doors. One, unlocked, gave upon the street in front of the night club with its milling confused throngs. The other seemed to lead to the orchestra dais. He turned back to the corpse.

Gasped, sickened exclamations rose as patrolmen and detectives looked down at the inert heap on the floor. Looking up, the Phantom saw the rugged face of Frank Havens. He had never seen the publisher so pale, so fraught with lines of utter horror and shock. Havens's eyes, stark and wide, were fixed in awful fascination on that inert heap.

The Phantom studied the body closely. His first brief glance had already determined that the man was Clyde Dickson, wealthy, gaunt owner of this club; and that Dickson was as dead as any man could be.

The corpse was sprawled on its back. The eyes stared up, sightless and glazed. The gaunt features of Clyde Dickson looked unreal, as if they were some frozen snapshot of a face caught in a moment of unutterable agony and terror. Beneath the disheveled mop of hair on the night club owner lay a small wet pool of crimson blood.

No bullet had killed Clyde Dickson. No knife had stabbed him. The Phantom saw now why the police were looking down sickened, and why, especially, Frank Havens was staring in such an uncanny, horrified manner.

For something dark and long was protruding from the top of the dead man's skull!

Van's own nerves went cold. His hand instinctively touched his pocket, where the torn drawing of the hapless Eddie Collins crackled. Incredibly, weirdly, a portion of that drawing had become accurately simulated by the corpse in this room! That one, torn face, with something blackish protruding from the head-something Havens had called an ink-stain!

Grim-eyed, the Phantom stepped forward, bent down. He saw the protruding thing for what it was. A broken length of iron crowbar. A crowbar, large and thick, had been driven somehow through the skull of Clyde Dickson-through scalp and bone, into the brains beneath!

"Good God!" Havens started to gasp in horror. The Phantom's mask flashed up blackly; through its holes his eyes darted a tacit command to the publisher. Havens quickly turned away, silent.

"Say, in all my time I never saw anything like this!" It was a square-jawed captain of detectives who spoke now, hoarsely. "Hell, we heard him being killed-but how could anyone drive a bar like that through a man's skull, all in seconds too! And what devil —"

Even as he voiced the chill question, the Phantom, eyes sharpening anew, quietly pointed to the floor, to a spot about a foot away from that gruesome, crowbar-riven head.

A small object lay there, hideously familiar to the police, though Van himself looked at it for the first time.

It was a white saber tooth!

"The Fang!" Several police voices chorused in grim unison. "The Fang again!"

Twice in one night, since the arrival of the *Charlemagne*, an elusive, diabolical murderer had struck-struck under the very noses of the police, leaving his flaunting mark of death! And his second crime outdid the first in sheer, bloody mutilation!

The detective captain bawled out, in fierce rage: "This Fang can't be far away, damn him! We've got his description! We must get him!"

His eyes swiveled to the broken window then, for, as if to answer his words, wearied bluecoats were climbing back in, shaking their heads. "No one in that dead-end alley," one reported. "And no one but a human fly could climb that wall."

"Or a human devil!" the captain added.

Van's voice, cool despite his inner tension, came like a sane note in the raw-nerved agitation. "The breaking window might well have been a bit of decoying," he suggested. "The criminal might have gone out that door to the street to mingle with the crowd. Or he might have re-entered the night club, using that other door concealed by the orchestra dais."

This sent the police hunting in new directions. Some went out to the street; others hurried into the night club proper, where the patrons and employees, here since the big holdup, still stood, huddled and frightened.

The Homicide Squad arrived in the next seconds, faces already wearied from the work of the first murder. The City Medical Examiner came with Inspector Gregg, detective chieftain, whose own placid face was now looking dull grey, his eyes bloodshot and haggard.

"So you're in the case, Phantom!" The inspector, after grimly viewing the corpse, faced the man in the domino mask. "Maybe you can help us out-though really this case seems open-and-shut. If only we can get our hands on Al Millett!" He swore harshly. "I've been getting headaches from reports from every precinct, and a lot of well-meaning cranks as well. Every Tom, Dick, and Harry has been taken for Millett-but the right man is still loose, running the big mob organized tonight. He seems to be getting a crazy revenge by robbing and killing in this mad way!"

Shaken, he glanced again towards the corpse. The Medical Examiner was kneeling over the dead man now, his face pale despite his familiar acquaintanceship with death. "Well, Doc?"

The examiner raised baffled eyes.

"Beats me!" he confessed, crisply. "The Marcy brothers case was bad enough-obviously killed with some sort of ax. But a crowbar—I never saw it used this way in a murder! Can't see how a man could be strong enough to smash it through the cranium!"

The Phantom spoke a quiet question. "Do you think the crowbar was driven in with one blow, Doctor?"

The doctor shook his head. "Can't tell how it was driven in, Phantom. The whole upper cranium is shattered; there was a bad internal hemorrhage."

Van turned to the inspector. "Can you offer any possible reason, inspector-from what those men told you at the pier-for the murderer killing in this fashion?"

The inspector wiped sick perspiration from his brow. "They claimed Millett had a grudge against them because they once refused to back him in a show. And that he had a criminal mind which ran amuck. That ballyhoo he used in his exhibitions twenty years ago, must be true-that he's a born criminal, a killer."

Van nodded, his eyes thoughtful as he listened to these theories.

Then, as fingerprint men and other experts of the Homicide took possession of the room, the Phantom, Havens, and the inspector strode out into the night club proper.

Here, other detectives had garnered a wealth of evidence from the frightened patrons and employees, who had not been informed of the murder so close at hand. They gave the inspector their reports.

The holdup itself had been quite orthodox. It had been led by a big man in a slicker with a tommy gun—a man identified by the police as Monk Gorman. The gangsters had shot out the chandelier and escaped through windows and doors when sirens sounded, someone having managed to summon the police.

No one had seen anybody go into the rear office, or out of it. The murder had apparently been an aftermath of the robbery in which jewels and money running into thousands, according to the claims of the victims, had been filched.

There was one queer element about the holdup, however. No one had seen the actual entrance of the gangsters. The reason was that all had been watching the girl on the trapeze.

Their eyes had literally been magnetized by that act, for at the moment the girl had been performing a daring somersault. Her grip on the trapeze had faltered, and it seemed she would fall.

Van's sharp eyes studied the dangling, studded trapeze he had noticed when he first entered.

"That was Queen Stella," the Phantom said aloud to the inspector. "The most remarkable aerialist of today, and rather a mystery herself. I wonder if she really faltered, or whether that wasn't just a clever part of her act."

The inspector had already quizzed the workers here. No one had seen Queen Stella since she was on the trapeze.

The inspector's eyes were narrowed. "Begins to look as if she sneaked out on us. And you say that losing her grip stuff might have been part of her act? Damned convenient if it was-it got everyone's eye when the holdup men came in."

The patrons of the night club were beginning to protest their detention. Presently one of them, a tall, dress-suited man, strode angrily forward to confront the inspector. Van's eyes went to him keenly. Tall, swarthy, with a short, but wide-spreading beard of black, bristly hair, he had a foreign aspect. His eyes were sharp and hard.

"May I ask permission to leave at once?" His English was flawless, the too-clear English which a well-educated foreigner speaks. "This detention is most distressing to me. To be robbed is enough."

The inspector eyed him in distaste. "Who are you?"

The man made a stiff little bow. "I am Count Karnov, formerly of the Russian Court —"

"Oh!" The inspector's smile was slightly depreciating, for ex-Russian counts, genuine and bogus, were all too prevalent on Broadway. "Well, I'm sorry, Count. We can't make any exceptions. Been in this country long?" he added, casually.

"Just long enough to learn," Count Karnov replied angrily, "that your customs are rather embarrassing."

Beard bristling, he bowed himself back to the other huddled guests.

The inspector sighed. "Guess I'll have to release 'em all soon now. Can't hold them all night-and we want to get the body out. We'll check up on them all as a matter of routine. What do you think, Phantom?"

"I think it's safe to let them go. But I'd keep tabs on Count Karnov if I were you."

The inspector cursed grimly. "Don't worry. We'll find out about him all right."

Minutes later the big night club was emptying. The patrons filed out like a mass of frightened sheep herded by bluecoat shepherds. The employees went home wearily.

Last to leave-only the Phantom, the police, and Havens remaining-was the gruesome, crowbar-riven corpse of Clyde Dickson. The body was carried out in a plain wicker basket, by two morgue attendants-carried humbly from the sumptuous club Clyde Dickson had owned.

Soon after, the detectives who still scoured the murder office emerged. They had found no significant clues-no prints save Dickson's own.

But the Phantom, though he fully trusted the efficiency of the police, was not satisfied with their reports. It was possible that with his own leads, leads known only to himself and Frank Havens, he might find something they had dismissed as insignificant.

Accompanied by Havens, Van stepped into the murder room. There was a single desk, full of papers which the detectives had obviously gone through. Nevertheless, Van proceeded to go through them again.

"Van!" Havens spoke freely now, as once more they were alone. "What do you make of all this? That cartoon of Collins has been haunting me ever since this murder! Why, Collins seemed to —"

"—prophesy this crowbar killing?" Van broke in, grimly, as he continued his search. "It almost seems so, doesn't it, Frank? Yes, Collins certainly was on to something vital to this whole devilish mystery. That's why I've got to see this case through to a finish, Frank." He spoke with gripping determination. "Collins took us in deep waters-and it's a case of sink or swim!"

"I can't make head or tail of it!" Havens confessed, baffled. "That weird story about Al Millett-the criminal of twenty years ago coming back and killing, robbing! It sounds mad!"

"It sounds theatrical," Van replied, his keen analytical mind showing its work now. "There's showmanship in these murders, if nothing else. The leaving of the fang-the sensational pulling of the crime right under the noses of the police. A devilish showman, this 'Fang.' And yet there must be a reason, Frank. The well-planned robberies, the organization of the gang by perfectly orthodox underworld tactics, shows cold-blooded planning! And something tells me that even the murder methods thus far used were based on sound, logical reason too."

"Reason!" Havens protested. "To rip the sides of two men out with an ax! To drive a crowbar through another man's skull! What reason could there be except what the men told the inspector-that Millett's mind is fiendishly warped, that he's been nursing a grudge and is now taking it out with homicidal fury."

"Perhaps," Van conceded. "Yet, somehow I'm not satisfied with that explanation. Frank, I want you to check up-in your news files and other sources-on all the men involved in this. See if you can bring anything to light."

He shook his head, still going through papers on the desk. "One thing else strikes me as strange. When I was trying to break into this room, I heard Dickson —I'm sure it was he-shriek out 'You! It's you!' in obvious recognition of the criminal."

"That isn't strange," Havens protested. "He simply recognized Al Millett."

"Yet, Frank, he sounded surprised-as well as terrified. Was he surprised to see Millett, knowing Millett was in town and at large? At any rate, did his recognition bring on his own murder?"

He broke off his grim musings as his fingers now thumbed through a small, frayed memorandum book he had found in Dickson's desk.

Its leather cover was peeling, worn at the edges. On its frayed pages, the Phantom saw scrawled names and addresses in faded ink, all of them business firms, mostly connected with entertainment. He thumbed on through the book. Suddenly, he paused at a fresh page-his eyes sharpening visibly in the holes of the domino mask.

"Look at this, Frank."

Havens looked. He saw what seemed at first a faint smudge of ink and alongside of it was an address, a number in the West Forties.

The faded ink showed it, too, had been jotted down long ago.

But Havens adjusted a pair of reading glasses and studied the item carefully under Van Loan's urging. He gave an exclamation. The smudge was a definite pattern, a clover-like outline.

"It's a design, Van! A sort of shamrock-no, not that —"

"Think of a deck of cards, Frank."

Havens eyes lighted with amazement. "Of course! It's the symbol for a club card! A card! And on that torn cartoon of Collins's there's a card, too: a joker under a skull. Do you think —"

"I think this symbol can be read as a word," Van's own voice held a gripping eagerness now. "What we have then is: Club, followed by an address." His body straightened now, eyes gleaming. "Club! And I've a hunch it might be the Gargoyle Club also mentioned in Collins's cartoon! It's pretty late-but I'm going there at once!"

Frank Havens wanted to go along, but Van, sensing danger now, feeling that the time had come to work undercover, insisted upon setting out alone. Turning over what evidence he had to Havens, and leaving instructions for Havens to check up on the men involved, also to try to obtain the murder-crowbar after the Medical Examiner finished his autopsy-the Phantom strode out of the Palladium Club.

A small but powerful coupe was already awaiting him at the side-street curb. Havens had phoned his chauffeur to speed that car here.

The Phantom moved like a shadow through the crowds that milled out here, keeping his mask low so the darkness virtually concealed it. Quickly, he slid into the coupe, stepped on the starter. The motor hummed.

The Phantom whirled in the seat in sudden alarm. Something whizzed in through the window of the car, falling upon his lap!

Grim-eyed, he now picked up the object that had been tossed in so surreptitiously. It was a note, wrapped around a small spoon from the Palladium. Delicate fine handwriting showed under the dashboard lights.

Phantom:

> *Anything you do will be a waste of time until you see me. If you really want to know of Al Millett, be at the corner of Bethune and Varick Streets tomorrow at six p.m. Come alone, or it will be useless. I knew you from your mask —*
>
> *Queen Stella.*

Queen Stella! The missing girl aerialist who had been drawing all eyes when the holdup began!

Van's eyes again went to the crowd, looking for the girl. At that instant a taxi pulled up to the curb. The Phantom saw a tall man with a cane climbing stiffly into it; caught a brief glimpse of a heavy-jowled pale face. The taxi-door slammed, the cab shot off around a corner, at a breathless speed.

But the Phantom had recognized its passenger. That man was Bernard J. Andrews, the big radio station owner! One of the men who had come to Inspector Gregg with the story of Al Millett! What was he doing, lurking around the night club where the Fang had struck a second time?

The Phantom's own car hurled from the curb even with these thoughts. He drove rapidly around the corner, onto Broadway, scanning the still-heavy night traffic. Andrews's cab was lost in a maze of other cabs.

Nor did he try to find it now. He also shoved away the note signed with the name of Queen Stella, his eyes grim. Anything he did, the note said, would be a waste of time until tomorrow.

He smiled to himself as he set out for the address he had picked up in Dickson's office: the address marked only with the symbol of the club-suit from a deck of cards.

Chapter VI
The Gargoyle Club

Night was finally in its small, dying hours. Eerie tendrils of mist seeped down the street east of Sixth Avenue, cooling the deserted pavements which slowly relinquished the Indian summer heat of the previous day.

The side street had a lonely aspect. Yet, close by, was plenty of life and activity. From Sixth Avenue came sounds that drowned out the occasional rumble of the elevated trains-sounds of drilling and pumping-now and then the dull boom of a blast. A subway line was under construction, being rushed with three eight-hour shifts every twenty-four hours.

But the side street here was aloof from the clamor. At the moment, there was no visible sign of anyone on the entire block. Yet someone was there.

Blending with the shadows of the dark building fronts, yet moving hurriedly along the street, stole the Phantom. He had left his coupe parked on another street.

His keen eyes glanced at each passing house number. And then they found that which they sought, and his lithe body slowed in its pace. This building made a strange contrast to the tall, modern office skyscrapers that rose like canyon walls on either side of the street. It was small, squat, of ancient brownstone, and was squeezed between two of the skyscrapers, as if it had defiantly refused to heed the march of time-had stubbornly remained when its neighbors had been torn down to make way for architectural progress.

From every appearance it was a tenantless house. Though no For Sale signs hung on it, its windows were partially boarded, a few others showing broken age-begrimed panes. Its door, too, had boards over it.

The Phantom felt a sense of disappointment. This was the address, marked by the symbol of a club, which he had found in Dickson's ancient book. And from the looks of it, the place was long since fallen into disuse, as defunct as the rest of the addresses in that book.

The Phantom glanced up and down the block. It was empty, deserted. Moving to the worn stoop of the dilapidated house, he ascended the stone stairs, came to the boarded door. The boards, he saw now, were nailed to the door behind them, a hole cut through where the key-hole of the lock showed.

The Phantom's interest quickened. That key-hole looked new. Again he glanced up and down the street, eyes darting through his mask-holes. No one in sight.

From a pocket he now took out a slender piece of wire. It looked quite ordinary. Actually it was of specially tempered steel, malleable, yet always able to recover its original shape. Into the key-hole the Phantom inserted the wire. His deft fingers manipulated it. No burglar could have been more swift and expert at picking that lock.

In just a moment, with scarcely a sound, the Phantom had the lock picked. Cautiously he swung the big boarded door on its hinges, slipped into the house, closing the door softly behind him.

The gloom that met him at first seemed opaque. A musty odor clogged his sensitive nostrils. He moved cautiously, on his soft-soled shoes, eyes gradually accustoming themselves to the darkness.

The ancient interior of the house slowly came into view. Gaping doorways, a rickety flight of stairs. The whole place seemed desolate and dead, a decayed relic of the past. Once, no doubt, it had been a fashionable house-its ornate fixings indicated that. But now it was only an archaic shell, and as he groped his way through it, the desolate emptiness of it seemed to engulf the Phantom like a weird, evil spell.

He felt as if he had stepped out of all modern civilization and progress into a world that no longer existed, a world that could only hold ghosts of the past.

Ghosts! Certainly the *Phantom* could laugh at the idea of ghosts! Yet, even with the thought, a slight, scurrying sound came to his ears. He dismissed it quickly, with a little shiver. Rats, no doubt.

Then, all at once, he heard another sound. His lithe body jerked rigid.

As if welling up vaguely from some invisible source there came a sound of voices.

Nerves taut, the Phantom listened with ears acutely tuned, trying to reckon their direction. But they came only as vague murmurings, and Van half-wondered if his imagination was not playing tricks on him.

He moved about. Again came that ghostly murmur. But this time his ears told him it had come from above. The stairs, he had already seen, were covered with fully half an inch of undisturbed dust! Nevertheless, the Phantom ascended them, his soft-soles treading lightly on their creaking wood.

He reached the second and top floor of the house. A musty hall, again gaping rooms whose dirt-grimed windows hid the city outside, shutting this ghastly place off from civilization. Certainly, the floor was absolutely vacant, empty.

Yet, at that very instant, the voices sounded again closer now. He caught a snatch of words —
"I'll see you in hell first!"

The speech came like a single, crackling explosion, then as instantly subsided, so that again Van couldn't be sure he had really heard them. Yet his every nerve told him something devilish was going on in this house.

The sound had come from close by, from the very top of the stair landing here. Yet there was no room here, just a wall, outside of which must be the street. He bent to the wall, fingers groping in the darkness-for he still dared show no light.

Suddenly his fingers touched metal, a small grille of oblong shape. In a flash he realized that it was one of the old-fashioned type of heat-grilles.

A slight draft came through it, but no light. Swiftly Van Loan comprehended. Those grilles made excellent sound conductors. The voices had come up between the walls from below.

Van moved again to the stairs, descended them. He came to the ground floor once more. His eyes, straining in the gloom, saw the side of the staircase now, saw how far outwards it extended. He hurried to it, Colt .45 whipping out, thumb snapping down the safety catch so that the weapon was ready for use.

He could hear nothing now, but his left hand groped along the wall of the staircase. A hunch had grown within him as he noticed the strange paneling here.

In the very next instant, near some coping, his hand was arrested by a small metal catch. With his other hand coming forward with his gun, the Phantom pressed that catch.

There was a click — a hissing swish.

Bright light momentarily dazzled the Phantom as it came flooding out toward him, grotesquely illuminating the ancient, dusty hallway, throwing weird shadows.

Gun leveled, eyes slitted in the holes of his black domino mask, the Phantom hurled his body through the revealed doorway and to one side.

A large, strange chamber was before him. It was empty.

He was certain even before his eyes located a grille near the ceiling that this was where the voices had come from. But there was no one in the room! Had those voices come from invisible ghosts?

His eyes took in the chamber. Oak-paneled walls, windowless — a luxurious and well-kept room, pleasantly illumined by modern indirect lighting. An amazing contrast to the rest of the dilapidated house.

There was a table in the center of the room, a long oak table with several chairs around it. Two were pulled out from the rest, indicating that they might have been hastily vacated.

The Phantom's eyes went wider. He had come through the secret doorway to this room. He was sure it hadn't been used by anyone since his arrival in the house. Had those voices been imaginary then? Or was there another exit?

His eyes were drawn hypnotically to one wall and a chill shock went through him, tightening his every nerve.

Leering at him from that wall was a human skull. Beneath it, pinned to form a pattern with it, was a playing card—a joker! The strange symbol he had found in that torn cartoon by Eddie Collins!

He moved back to the table. Nothing on it. If only there were some clue as to who had been in here. He stiffened anew. There *was* something on the table. Or, rather, in the table's oak surface. A bronze plaque was inlaid at the head. Van bent over it.

Nine names were inscribed in that plaque, well known names that seemed to leap out like letters of blood before his eyes! Nine names he had heard at the very outset of this strange case.

> Benjamin Marcy
> Lyle Marcy
> Gordon Drake
> Bernard J. Andrews
> Carl Fenwick
> Clyde Dickson
> Paul Corbin
> Kenneth Meade
> John Gifford

The mighty moguls of the amusement world, three of whom had just been killed! Here, in this room, under the symbol of the skull and joker, they apparently had held secret meetings. For what reason-if they had no past to hide, no secret?

Grim-eyed now, realizing that he had come to some vital core of the mystery if he could but interpret it, the Phantom proceeded to examine the secret room.

He found something else that caught his attention. On another wall, near the secret panel he had entered, had hung what had evidently been a large placard of some sort. Now just a corner of it remained, frayed and dusty. Printing, in an archaic type long since gone out of use, revealed three letters:

kil

The unfinished word seemed to blend with that leering skull across the room, and if ever Van felt the presence of menace, of death itself, he felt it at the very instant he gazed at that strange, mutilated sign.

At that instant the sixth sense which the Phantom possessed leaped once more to the fore. Certainly he had not heard the slight, cautious sound behind his back. He hadn't expected it, because he had already surveyed the entire room, and now he was facing the secret door through which he himself had come.

Only when his muscles were already whirling his body, his hand whipping up his gun, did he feel the draft of air from behind him, a draft which told him some other door must have opened. But even as he whirled, eyes sharp, the lights of the room went out!

The windowless chamber was plunged into Stygian darkness. The Phantom, though he could see nothing, was acutely aware of a shape charging toward him! His whole body braced. But, despite his forewarning of it, the Phantom was almost bowled completely over by the savage ferocity of the body which hurled against his own, knocking his gun from his fist. Hands reached for his throat, hands that were like vises of steel. In the darkness he struggled with his powerful antagonist, tugging at the hands which had closed on his wind-pipe and were choking the breath from his lungs.

Rallying his strength, the Phantom was matching his adversary with the strength and skill of self-defense he had practiced arduously. Something struck Van's back as his antagonist momentarily forced him against the wall. A light-switch, he was certain!

Gathering strength, he twisted his antagonist around. One hand had released the awful, choking pressure on his throat-he could breathe again. He gave a yank, freeing momentarily his left hand. Fiercely, he reached for the switch. Light would reveal that face. More than anything else, that was what Van wanted to see.

But even as his groping fingers touched the switch a sudden, rasping shout broke from his still-unseen attacker.

"Men! Over here! He's the Phantom!"

Almost simultaneously, Van heard a heavy rush of feet from the secret door he himself had entered. With a curse of alarm, he whirled as his antagonist now jerked away.

Now his eyes were able to discern several shadowy figures, groping for him. Rough hands reached out, grabbing at him. The Phantom struck out blindly with his own powerful fists, but there were too many for him now. Blows cuffed him. He heard an awful, swishing sound-the sound of a heavy black-jack arcing viciously through the air. His very brain seemed to explode, causing myriad colors to dance before his eyes.

Stunned, he fought to keep consciousness while hands frisked him in the dark-frisked him but failed to find one item that, by a secret legerdemain on Van's part, always defied ordinary search-the diamond-studded platinum badge of the Phantom!

In the next moment the lights went on. Blinking, the Phantom again took in the strange chamber.

There were five slouch-hatted men in the room. Three of them, yanking him to his feet and covering him with guns, he recognized at once as the thugs who had attacked him when he had posed as Collins. There was the broken-nosed thug called Gus with tape on his wrist which had been wounded. There was the hatchet-faced gunman, and the pallid one.

One more slouch-hatted figure was a stranger. The fifth, standing at the light switch, was a burly man in a sport-belted slicker. Van's eyes narrowed with swift recognition. Monk Gorman!

But where was the man who had originally attacked the Phantom single-handed, then given orders to this gang? Van was sure he was not one of these thugs.

As this thought flashed through the Phantom's mind, the big man in the slicker came striding over.

"So you're the Phantom," he sneered, glaring with hate at the masked man who had awed the underworld. "Well, this time you bucked something too big for you, pal."

Gus snarled then. "Say Monk-why waste time?" Despite his taped wrist he leveled his automatic toward Van, eyes alight with murder. "Let me give him a belly-full o' slugs, will ya, Monk? Hell, he's probably the guy who potted my wrist and wounded Pete when he got that envelope —"

Van stiffened as the automatic pointed its black muzzle towards him. Though his strength was not yet returned, he did not intend to die without a struggle.

"Hold it, hold it!" Monk commanded, pushing Gus aside. "We ain't doin' anythin' in here! Just one thing before we get goin' with this Phantom bird, let's have a good look at him!"

Van, menaced by guns, unarmed, did not try to make resistance, even though he saw Monk's intent!

Deliberately now, with evil satisfaction in his bead-like eyes, Monk's paw-like hand reached forward. It seized the edge of the domino mask. A savage rip-and the mask came off.

But it did not reveal the face of Richard Curtis Van Loan, a face that would have shown through the scant disguise of Eddie Collins. Before he had come to this building, Van, with keen precaution, had put on a new and strong make-up —a disguise which altered his features into those of a hard-looking man of indeterminate age.

"So that's what you really look like, Phantom?" Monk seemed disappointed, as if he expected to see some super-being. "Hell! I never seen your puss before. All right, we'll get goin'! Tony, bring that over!"

The pallid-faced thug came forward with a length of stout cord. In a matter of seconds the Phantom was bound hand and foot, arms pinioned behind him. His mouth was taped.

Monk barked a fresh order. They picked the bound Phantom up and started toward the secret panel.

"No, not that way, Choppy!" Monk rapped. "Might be coppers out front, an' I'm hot!" He moved to the opposite wall, where he pressed a catch.

Another secret panel, in that wall, slid open. The Phantom was carried through it into a dark, tunnel-like passage. The panel was closed behind as Monk followed.

A long journey through the dark passage which descended slightly and then rose. The faintly cool air of the misty outdoors engulfed the Phantom. He realized they had emerged on the next block downtown from the house. The passage, evidently some old drainage duct, afforded a direct route from the secret room to the street, leading out through the cellar of another house.

But who had been the man who cried: "I'll see you in hell first"? Who had been the powerful brute who had attacked Van Loan in the dark? Was the Phantom going to learn the answers to these questions?

Chapter VII
A Narrow Escape

Carried to a large sedan, the captive Phantom was tossed like a sack into the rear. Tony leaped into the front seat, got the motor going. Another thug slid alongside him. Monk, Gus, and the hatchet-faced man named Choppy climbed in roughly over Van's half-doubled figure, trampling him brutally down to the floorboards.

"Where we takin' this Phantom bird, Monk?" the broken-nosed Gus demanded, a note of awe in his tones. "Gonna take him to the new 'chateau' so the Boss can —"

"Shut up!" Monk snarled. "Tony, drive like I told you."

The Phantom, gathering strength to struggle as best he could against his bonds, relaxed, grim hope in his heart as the sedan rolled on. Helpless and bound though he was, he wished they would take him to that unknown destination, to the lair of the Fang!

And then the sedan rolled to a stop.

All this time, on the sides of the avenue, below the elevated, Van had been aware of the noisy clamor of the subway excavating. Now the din had reached a climax. The car had turned a little way into another dim side street. Monk alone climbed out.

He was gone several minutes. Then, hurriedly, his slouch-hatted head again poked into the car.

"Okay, guys! Bring him out. Follow me and be careful! If there's any trouble, use your rods!"

Again the Phantom was lifted bodily. Out of the car the four others took him, and trotted with him along the quiet street.

Bright arc-lights appeared on the avenue, where drills and compressors shattered the final hours of the night. There was a deep excavation, extending to a vacant lot here. Workmen swarmed in it. A huge derrick was steaming and straining in the center.

With a boldness that astonished the bound Phantom, his captors carried him down an incline into that excavation. Monk was signaling them on.

The workmen were all preoccupied, watching the derrick, whose great arm was lifting a dark, massive burden.

"Here-put him here! Hurry!"

They dragged the Phantom over rough, uneven, rocky ground. Suddenly, he was dropped violently. His bound body banged against the slanting surface of a heavy, sand-covered rock. Stunned again, his every bone shaken, he could not move.

As they dropped him, all five thugs scurried away like hasty fleeing rats.

Van, twisting up his head, saw —

The derrick arm was lowering. Its shadow was right above him. He saw the massive burden it was bringing down. A huge net of steel!

It was right on top of him, coming like a huge blanket. Somewhere to the right the workmen were guiding it by long ropes. They did not see him here in the gloom, nor could he shout to them with the tape over his mouth!

Down came the steel net. The Phantom braced his body, flattening as best he could against the rock, as his last effort to roll out of the way of the great expanse of net proved futile.

Then it was on him. Its crushing weight knocked the breath anew from his lungs. Steel links and cables bruised through his clothes, dug into his flesh. It was lucky he was not crushed to death.

Lucky? Even as the steel net flattened over him and the rock now, and the derrick swung away with empty jaws Van knew that he had not escaped death. This was but a grim preparation for it!

A vague figure out in the gloom, evidently a foreman, was yelling, "Clear away, men! This is gonna be a whopper!"

Simultaneously Van's eyes, jerking to one side, caught a faint outline of electric wires, going into the rock close beside him. There were two other rocks nearby, also covered with nets.

His blood chilled as he comprehended the diabolical intention of the murderous Monk Gorman. Instead of taking him to the "chateau," they had planned a ghastly doom for him! These three rocks were loaded with dynamite. They were about to be blasted. The nets that covered them were to keep the explosion as confined as possible, so the shattered rock would not erupt all over the place.

Three rocks to be blasted! And on the center one, pinned down by that steel net, lay the Phantom. In a moment now he would be blown to bits, his body torn beyond all means of identification! It was a devilishly clever means of getting rid of him, of removing him from the bizarre murder case without leaving a tangible clue.

"Come on, men, hurry up!" the foreman was shouting. Obviously he stood at the hand-detonator, ready to send the current through the wires to the fulminate caps packed in the dynamite. "Clear away, I say!"

Van had spent precious seconds trying to shout, but it was useless. The adhesive remained tight over his lips. Now, knowing that only seconds remained, he fought to keep calm in the face of the ghastly predicament!

In that swift moment, his muscles strained tentatively, feeling for any place where the pressure was not impossibly heavy. His left arm behind him was partially protected by the hollow of his back.

The Phantom had made a thorough study of escapes. He had analyzed the escapes of the late Houdini, until he had mastered similar tricks. Now he applied every bit of knowledge he could summon to this crisis.

His wrist twisted, muscles flexing and unflexing in his forearm.

"All clear?" The foreman was shouting.

The words spurred the Phantom's efforts. He gave a sudden peculiar jerk, with all his strength. His arm, with rope still clinging to it, came free.

Just one arm, his left, to work with at all-and the blast about to go off! But the Phantom had already gauged his one possible chance of escape from death.

The electric feed wires! With all his strength he pushed his arm out from behind him, his body heaving against the steel net, managing to push it upwards just a trifle, though the effort made every muscle groan in protest.

He couldn't see the foreman. Yet, as if his intuition had eyes, he could envision the man even now stooping to push the plunger.

An inch more! With one last effort he made it. His fingers seized both wires and yanked.

Br-r-rooooom!

The whole world seemed to detonate about his ears, leaving him deaf! Smoke and fire leaped about him. He felt the rock shiver under his spine.

But his rock had not been blasted! The two other rocks had disintegrated, gone up in that net-stifled upheaval! The wires to this rock, which he had ripped in that last split second from the fuse-caps, had not carried the current to the fatal dynamite sticks. A moment later cautious workmen appeared above Van's net carrying lanterns and coming to see why the dynamite had failed to detonate. Their cries of amazed surprise and alarm faintly sounded in Van's pained ears as their lamps revealed the pinned figure under the net.

They had to use the derrick to remove the heavy expanse of steel. Hands helped Van to his feet. Voices shouted questions at him. Someone ran to summon an ambulance.

But the Phantom was not there when the ambulance came. Bruised and shaken, he had paused only to recapture his lost wind, his ebbed strength.

Then, so quickly that the workmen were left gasping, he whirled from the group, darted across the gloom of the excavation, and disappeared in the misty dawn which was just breaking over the city.

* * *

"Yes, Frank, the criminal was at that Gargoyle Club or I miss my guess. And he knew I was the Phantom."

Morning sunlight slanted warmly through the French windows of Havens's office in the *Clarion* Building, as the Phantom, refreshed by clean clothes, medical treatment at the hands of his valet, and nourishment, sat beside the publisher's desk.

Havens's face showed the deep-lined strain of a sleepless night, mingled with the relief at seeing the Phantom safe and sound.

"The police went to that club, as you call it, as soon as you phoned, Van," he reported. "They found the secret room. But the name plaque you mentioned wasn't there; nor was that torn sign on the wall."

Van's eyes were grim. "Evidently they were removed by the criminal. Guess he attacked me because I saw them. I wonder what —" He broke off with a shrug, lit a cigarette thoughtfully. "Any other developments, Frank?"

"Yes. The police have been checking up on all the people present in the Palladium Club during that holdup. One of them, that man who called himself Count Karnov, seems to interest them. As far as they can make out, he arrived only recently in this country-and he's been moving fast from hotel to hotel. They're trying to check up on him. Queen Stella is still missing. And nothing known about her identity, either."

Van smiled grimly. He did not tell Havens about the note he had in his pocket, signed by the trapeze artist's sobriquet. He had left that note in the coupe when he had gone to the Gargoyle Club. Later, after his hectic adventure, he had found the coupe intact. But he kept the note to himself now, aware that it might still be a false lead, a red herring which might confuse the trail. But the memory of the wording of it —*"Anything you try to do will be a waste of time —"* brought a queer thrill to the Phantom. His visit to that strange house of the secret room had been far indeed from a waste of time.

"About this Al Millett, Frank," he spoke aloud. "Is it true he used to give some of his exhibitions for a circus-Crowley and Buckle's once-famous circus?"

"Yes, among other road shows. Why, Van?"

"I want you to get me all the data you can on that circus, Frank," the Phantom demanded without replying to the question. "Everything that might carry any information. I take it, you've already got some data on the men involved?"

Havens nodded. "A slew of stuff—I'm having it assembled. But I'm afraid it won't be of much value, Van. Those men have all been in the amusement business a long time. And as far as their careers go back publicly, there is nothing dark or hidden about them. Yet," he added, frowning thoughtfully, "they have one thing in common-their shunning of publicity. All are bachelors, living alone-except the murdered Marcys, who lived together. None of them seems to have any living relatives."

Van drew a puff of smoke, thinking as Havens spoke, of that mysterious room at the Gargoyle Club, the name plaque, those two voices-one heavy, and the other dry.

"If there are no relatives, who are the heirs of the estates of the murdered men?" he asked, interested.

"Their moneys are willed to charities, Van, institutions for the infirm-reputable places needing endowments. No one gains by their deaths except these institutions. Dickson and the Marcy brothers had practically all their wealth in their show places. But these are to be sold, the proceeds to be used in the settlement of their wills."

The publisher shook his head, sighed. "So you see, there isn't much to go by there. And I still can't see how Eddie Collins drew practically Dickson's murder before it happened." Grimly, his eyes went to the now empty lounge where the youthful cartoonist had died the night before.

"You looked through Collins's office stuff here? Checked up?" Van demanded.

"Yes. We found some scraps of comic cartoons-nothing much there. But I did find some peculiar scribblings, Van. They scarcely seem to make sense. I have them here."

He handed Van Loan some small pages, on which was bold handwriting. Van looked through them. His brows arched in surprise.

Bee doesn't die by sting-Red Sea is red as blood —

Van looked up, his eyes sharp, his mind racing.

"What is it, Van?" Havens demanded, noting the Phantom's absorption. "Do you see something there? It isn't, perhaps, some sort of code?"

"No, I don't think so," Van replied slowly. And slowly a light began to shine in his eyes. His voice was gripping now. "Frank—I'm beginning to see something! Something which is still without any definite pattern-but it's there-if only I can get a few more leads to it! And I'm pretty sure I know how Collins got mixed up in this!"

Havens stared at him, wide-eyed, accustomed though he was to the Phantom's often-amazing conclusions. "Van, what do you mean?"

"I'll tell you as soon as I'm a little more sure," Van returned. "And —" He broke off as the inter-office buzzer sounded.

"Beg pardon, Mr. Havens," the pleasant voice of the editor's secretary came from the speaker. "A Mr. Carl Fenwick wishes to see you. Says it is very urgent."

"Fenwick!" Havens repeated, glancing at Van Loan and observing his quick nod. "Send him in, please."

Van Loan swiftly turned up his collar and snapped a new domino over his face. Glancing swiftly around to be sure there were no traces of Richard Van Loan, he turned to study the newcomer.

Carl Fenwick, the man who looked almost like a clergyman because of his high, straight collar, came in with a nervous stride. His mild face was pale, fraught with agitation. His troubled eyes at first did not see the masked Phantom. "Mr. Havens," Fenwick said tensely. "Sorry if I've disturbed you. But I understand you can contact the man known as the Phantom! And —" He broke off, starting, as his glance now took in the domino-masked figure.

"You —I beg your pardon!" Fenwick stammered. "Are you —"

Van nodded grimly. "Yes, I'm the Phantom."

Fenwick gave a dry, mirthless, rather shaky laugh. "How-how fortunate, finding you here."

The Phantom said nothing to this; but inwardly he wondered if Fenwick meant those words. Was Fenwick surprised to see the Phantom alive? Had he perhaps come here to see if he *were* alive? Van had not forgotten that murderous attack in the secret room.

"Won't you sit down, Mr. Fenwick?" Havens invited now.

Fenwick nodded his thanks, took one of the comfortable chairs. He seemed to await a question from the Phantom. Van deliberately made none, coolly lighting another cigarette. He had already decided on his course of action: Carl Fenwick would have to take the initiative.

Fenwick tugged a little at his high collar. A moment of silence filled the room. Havens had already become a silent spectator, waiting at his desk. Then Fenwick leaned towards the Phantom. "I had to come to you, Phantom," he said, a haunting light in his eyes. His words came in a sudden rush, like a pent-up dam released. "I had heard, through the police, you were interested in this case. We went to the police, and they didn't help us. Now I'm coming to you. The others might not approve of it, but there's something I'm going to tell you."

Havens stiffened, scenting news. The Phantom remained cool, his eyes alone betraying his interest through the mask. Then he spoke dryly. "You mean," he said, "that you and others actually did do a real wrong to Millett."

Fenwick gasped and winced.

"No-no," he protested. "What we told Inspector Gregg was the truth. We simply refused to back Al Millett in a show of his own. As a result, he went broke. His wife died, and he disappeared. But there's more to the story. Millett and his wife had a child —a girl child who disappeared with Millett after the death of his wife."

The Phantom did not appear shocked or profoundly affected by this bit of information. He studied the theatrical producer thoughtfully for a moment. Then: "Very interesting, Mr. Fenwick," he said. "But just how, may I ask, does this item of personal history bear on this case?"

Fenwick tugged uncomfortably at his collar. "I—I don't know," he faltered. "I thought you ought to be told everything. Andrews, particularly, was opposed to my saying anything."

Van Loan remained thoughtful. Andrews was the radio company man, the chap the Phantom had seen walking away from the Palladium Club late last night after the murder of Dickson.

"Thank you, Mr. Fenwick," Van Loan acknowledged gravely. "I will remember what you have said."

The theatrical man, after a word of effusive thanks that the Phantom was on the case, took his leave.

"Well, Van?" The publisher asked. "What do you make of Fenwick's story?"

"Very little," Van admitted. "I believe him-certainly. But I still think there is a great deal more to this whole mess than any of them have told. Perhaps a talk with Bernard J. Andrews would be enlightening. Call Inspector Gregg on your private wire, Frank, and see where we can find the man right now. Gregg should know."

Havens quickly got the chief of detectives on the phone. His conversation with the inspector was brief. Turning back to the expectant Phantom, he exploded a bombshell.

"Van, Andrews has disappeared! He apparently slipped away from his home during the night. No signs of violence. He's just gone. There's an alarm out for him right now."

The Phantom stood erect. "Good-by, Frank. That means I've plenty of work to do. Get that information together for me and send it over to the lab as soon as you can."

And he was gone.

Chapter VIII
Queen Stella Again

Located in an old loft building was a queer business belonging to an eccentric recluse who went by the name of Dr. Bendix.

Neither the police nor the impoverished inhabitants of the lower East Side dreamed that, in the midst of the city's most squalid tenement section, there existed perhaps the finest and most fully equipped private crime-laboratory in the world.

The mysterious Dr. Bendix stood in that gleaming laboratory now, over a table full of retorts and test tubes.

Alone, he wore no mask or disguise. And friends of Richard Curtis Van Loan, the socialite, would have been amazed to see him hard at work here, in a stained smock, a cigarette dangling from his lips. That Richard Van Loan was "Dr. Bendix," that this was just another role of the Phantom, was a secret known only to Frank Havens.

Strange objects lay on the work-table before the Phantom. A broken iron crowbar. Two saber teeth. They had been sent here by Havens, who had obtained them from the Medical Examiner and the police department.

With a pair of tongs, Van heated the crowbar over the blue-white flame of a Bunsen burner. He dipped it, hissing, into a container of chemicals. His analysis was long and thorough. An analysis to get the blood of Clyde Dickson from the crowbar. To test the effect of the blood's oxygen content on the iron.

When at last he had finished, he had reached some strange conclusions. The crowbar was old-very many years old. Even the break in it did not look new. Why had the criminal who called himself the Fang taken an old, broken crowbar as a murder weapon? Van's eyes gleamed.

Of the Marcy brothers, whose sides had been ripped and mutilated, Van had no evidence of any weapon, but he had read the full, and baffled, autopsy report.

He gave his attention next to the saber teeth. He decided, by comparison with zoological books he had, that they were really the teeth of tigers. They could have been bought in any store selling trinkets of this sort.

The Phantom now moved from the work-table to a flat-topped desk. Here were the sheaves of newspaper clippings and other reports on the men involved in the case. Smoking thoughtfully, Van went through them.

The names of all the living men, with their corresponding dossiers, passed like a parade before the Phantom: Bernard J. Andrews, missing radio man-Gordon Drake-Carl Fenwick-Paul Corbin, night-club owner-John Gifford, amusement park manager.

The reports confirmed what Havens had already told him. But Havens had, in response to Van's request, sent one additional piece of information. Through his influence he had learned, from various law-firms, of the wills of all the rest of the men.

And like the murder victims, all of them were leaving their wealth to charities! Where the first victims had their money tied up in businesses that had to be liquidated, the rest had most of their fortune in sound Wall Street investments and in cash deposits.

It did not seem surprising. None had relatives, so it could be understood that they were leaving their wealth to public institutions. But it certainly seemed to offset any mercenary motive for their murder. They could have been robbed without being killed.

The Phantom rose, paced, brooding on his thoughts. It wasn't money that tied these men together. There was some bond which that mysterious club indicated. It didn't seem to be any dark or shady deed of the past. What, then? *What?*

Again that vague germ of light was in his brain. But it defied definition. Could the bond merely be a mutual fear of Al Millett-the Fang? No, for openly they had gone to the police confessing to such a bond while they had been darkly secretive about the Gargoyle Club. It was queer, the feeling Van had, the intangible feeling that as yet the right answer had not been found.

The Gargoyle Club-Van stopped on that thought, memory coming to him. He moved to a telephone, put in a call to the Department of Buildings. He asked for an official of high standing.

"This is Mr. Frank Havens," he said in the next moment, simulating perfectly the voice of the publisher who had given him full license to use this identity over the phone. "I called you before, if you remember, for a favor. Did you find out about the ownership of that old building on Forty-Fifth Street, near Sixth?"

"Yes, Mr. Havens," came the official's polite voice. "It belongs to a corporation-the Star Corporation. A Mr. John Gifford is president."

Gifford! The amusement park owner.

"That's a good piece of real estate, isn't it?" Van asked conversationally.

"Good indeed! You know how values have sky-rocketed in that section since Rockefeller Center was put up near there."

"Funny they don't develop the property."

"Yes, isn't it? I understand, too, they've had several juicy offers for it, but they refuse to sell."

When Van hung up, his eyes were keen, hard. Again he resumed his pacing. The ring of a bell at the end of the room brought him out of his musings. He waited a full moment, then went down the stairs to a foyer of the old loft. A package was waiting there, a big bundle of papers. Van knew that Havens's trusted office boy had delivered them, rung the bell, and quickly departed. His face eager, he carried the stuff upstairs, undid it on a table. It was the data he had been waiting for on the once famous Crowley and Buckill's circus.

Frank Havens, with his usual dependability, must have scoured the town to get such a mass of stuff. Some of the papers were frayed and decaying-their print archaic. In his preliminary examination, Van Loan pulled out of the stack an old three-sheet show bill.

He read the entire poster with careful attention.

Crowley & Buckill
GREATEST CIRCUS ON EARTH
Featuring the World's Largest
MUSEUM OF LIVING FREAKS!

Presenting the Famous Outlaw
AL MILLETT-THE FANG!

IN ADDITION
100 CLOWNS!
100 ACROBATS!
100 WILD ANIMALS
*SEE SIGNORINA BEATRICE,
THE WORLD'S GREATEST AERIALIST!*

Free Parade!

BAND OF 30 PIECES!

PLAYING HERE

There was a blank space for a dated streamer. But Van Loan's eyes went back to the first line-to the word "Buckill." With his hand he blocked off three letters-kil-and he knew what placard had been torn from the wall at the Gargoyle Club.

44

He spent the entire afternoon going through the stack of yellow and aging papers. He found individual posters on Al Millett's billing which described the fellow as a terror on wheels-followed by a thirty-piece band. There were single sheets on Signorina Beatrice, on the side shows, on the freak museum, on the animal tent, and so on. In their day Crowley and Buckill, like the Barnum who had preceded them, had been exploiting showmen. Van heaved a regretful sigh. This was like a trip back to childhood, to the sawdust paradise of the circus of yesteryear.

* * *

Dusk.

A tumble-down, desolate street near the Hudson River water-front. Just a few buildings and vacant lots. One lamp-post, its light having just gone on, was casting a dull glow in the thickening gloom.

The Phantom deliberately avoided that light.

In the shadows against the old buildings, he moved toward the corner of Bethune Street, domino mask once more on his face. His eyes were tense and alert; his right hand, which seemed to hang idly at the wrist, was ready to reach for his gun.

He was obeying the instructions in the note signed by the missing aerialist "Queen Stella." For there was a possibility the lead might prove bona-fide. He could not afford to pass it up.

The street, he saw, was empty. But it was not yet quite six-the hour of the rendezvous. Van neared the corner, saw that it formed the angles of an empty lot full of refuse-cans, garbage, wrecked autos.

It was then that a tension began to come over his nerves. A sense of danger.

He paused in the shadows, hesitating to step to the corner, where he would not only be revealed by the street-lamp, but also, with that open lot there, would be unshielded by any buildings. It was too perfect for a rub-out to suit the Phantom.

From where he stood, his eyes searched across the lot. Nothing in that refuse, he was sure. A slight movement that startled him proved to be a prowling alley cat.

Then his eyes went across the lot, to the rear of a dilapidated old building. It looked vacant, broken windowed. Because he was looking for it, he saw it then!

A broken lower window, something glinting over its sill —a round, dark muzzle! A gun ready to aim-and blast!

He sucked in a sharp breath, realizing that only his prescience had stopped him from walking out into the open before that waiting muzzle.

Then his eyes went to slits in their mask-holes. Grim purpose tightened his lips. He changed from the quarry to the hunter.

It was still a few minutes short of six.

The Phantom turned and went swiftly back from the corner. He slipped completely around the block, staying under cover, drifting like a dark mist to the front of that house on the next block.

Vacancy signs hung on it.

Half the front was torn down.

The brick walls were jagged and wrecked.

No one was in front of the house. There were no cars. No doorways where an ambusher could lurk unseen.

The Phantom approached the gaping front door of the house as stealthily as a cat.

The only sound he made was the slight click when his thumb pressed back the safety-catch on his Colt .45.

Like a wraith, he stole into the house. It was so ripped apart that he could see its emptiness. Toward the rear he saw that one door, on a single hinge, stood ajar. The Phantom peered in cautiously.

There in the twilight gloom a slouch-hatted figure crouched at that broken window over an automatic rifle which, Van saw by its extra coiled drum, had been converted into a machine gun.

From the portion of his sharp profile which the Phantom could see, Van knew that the would-be sniper was the hatchet-faced thug called Choppy.

The Phantom's slitted eyes narrowed in their purpose. He would get the truth from that felon in there, find out how this ambush had been pre-arranged. And why?

Cautiously, he moved the door. Then his breath sucked in. Despite his caution, the door creaked on its single hinge. There was nothing for it save to push on boldly in. He did so, whipping up his pistol.

Simultaneously, Choppy started. As he turned, his husky voice spoke:

"That you, Monk? That Phantom bird hasn't —"

He broke off in mid-sentence, hatchet-face blanching. For now he saw the domino-masked face coming toward him.

Coming like a grim Nemesis which every outlaw dreaded and secretly feared.

With a snarl of frightened rage, the thug snatched up the automatic rifle.

Desperation gave him almost superhuman speed. The barrel, sawed off in front, swung around and loomed blackly toward Van.

Crack!

It was the deep bark of the Phantom's Colt that shattered the empty, half-wrecked house. Van fired as he would at a desperate, dangerous beast.

The thug named Choppy seemed to freeze like a stone statue. Then the gun slanted crazily, clattered to the floor. And Choppy slowly slumped down after it, the life gone from his glazing eyes as he sprawled in a heap.

Grim-eyed, the Phantom moved forward. He glanced through the window. No one in sight. The shot evidently had not been heard-the rumble of trucks on West Street was enough to drown out more than one gun.

He looked down at the dead thug. He felt no sympathy for the felon, but he was sorry he had been forced to kill. Now his mind worked swiftly, to adjust to the grim situation. A glance at his wrist-watch showed it was just short of six o'clock. Outside the night was gathering.

Choppy had thought Van was Monk, the gang-leader, coming in here. Obviously he expected Monk, or others of the gang. But Van doubted that this old house could be the "chateau" the gunmen had mentioned last night. It was not a good hideout. It was only an ambush. Yet, perhaps any moment now, other gangsters would show up.

A grim decision came to Van then. It was six o'clock, and the fact that Queen Stella had not shown up made him feel the whole thing had been a trick to get him here.

He had turned the tables. Dared he go one step further, a step that might actually enable him to get directly on the trail of the criminal he sought?

His thoughts rapidly turned into swift action. He dragged the corpse of Choppy across the floor. It was still light enough to see, and he got more illumination when, once more, he drew out his flat make-up kit, snapped open the mirrored lid.

The corpse became his model, a model he now set out to reproduce on his own face with all his skill at disguise. Long, carefully drawn shadows gave his cheeks the hollows which made them look narrow and hatchet-like. A tiny bit of spring wire pinched his nostrils together, making them sharp and pointed like those of the thug. A cream-dye, rubbed into his hair, gave it Choppy's mousy color.

He took Choppy's clothes then, got into them. The blood-stain on the coat was small; he covered it with some more make-up. The clothes were tight, but he managed to pull them on, managed to put Choppy's slouch hat over his own head.

Hiding the corpse was his next problem. He solved it quickly. In the interior of the house, he found a corner piled with refuse. Minutes more, and he had Choppy's body screened behind it, hidden safely enough for the time being.

Again he slipped back to the rear room and peered out the window. His lips clamped back a sudden surprised exclamation.

Across the lot, under the lamp at the corner, apparently waiting, stood the slender figure of a girl! The aerialist had come to the rendezvous after all.

Van's mind raced. Was she actually intended as the bait for the trap, or was she innocent? In which case the gangsters must have learned of her rendezvous with the Phantom, and tried to turn it to their advantage.

In any event, the Phantom could not throw away this opportunity to meet the girl who had been missing since that murder at the Palladium Club.

Reaching a quick decision, he pulled his slouch hat a little lower, slipped out of the house the way he had come in. Again he circled the block warily, once more approaching the corner where the lamp-light cast its aura.

The girl was standing there, looking up and down the street anxiously. She wore a thin white summer coat, a halo hat. There was grace in every line of her slender body. But there was tension, too. Her white-gloved hands tugged at her purse.

The Phantom moved, unseen by her, until he was at the very fringe of the lighted corner-in the shadow of the last building there.

Then, low and soft, in a voice that was noncommittal, he called, "Queen Stella!"

Chapter IX
"Choppy" Investigates

Starting, the girl whirled. Her delicately featured, oval face showed whitely beneath auburn hair. For a moment she was confused, frightened.

Then she saw the vague figure standing in the gloom.

She stepped closer. But Van kept his slouch-hatted head down so she could not see him clearly.

"You came —" she almost questioned in a taut voice. It was impossible to tell from her tone whether she was grateful or not. But evidently she assumed he was the Phantom, for her words rushed on:

"You must not try to detain me. There is one thing I must tell you. It's about Al Millett —"

"Yes?" he prompted as she hesitated, his voice non-committal.

Her words came out passionately now; "Al Millett is not the fiend the police think! He was just a good actor-that's all! A charlatan, call him!"

Van's eyes narrowed. How did this girl-who could not be more than in her early twenties-talk so surely about Al Millett? And her voice was desperate, pleading, he noticed.

"You must believe me," she almost sobbed. "You must not hunt him down like a rat."

As she spoke she was shaking her purse, a white purse that gleamed in the light. It might have been purely nervousness, but on the other hand —"You and the police are wasting time seeking Al Millett. He isn't —"

The Phantom moved with the speed of lightning!

He had felt, rather than heard, the stealthy steps on the pavement. Now he saw dark shadowy figures, saw automatics whipping up toward his own figure.

Instantly he leaped past the girl, directly into the light of the street-lamp which shone upon his made-up face!

He knew that at that instant he was closer to death than he had ever been before. He knew that if his disguise were imperfect, if there were any flaw-Behind him now he heard the click-click of running high heels. The girl-running away! But he had no time for her now. Those revolvers were leveled right at him.

Then, "Hold it, guys! Hell, it's Choppy!" snarled the voice of Monk Gorman.

Van now turned around in feigned surprise which hid his relief. He saw the big, slickered gang leader coming forward with lowering gun. Saw the broken-nosed Gus, the pallid-faced Tony, and one other capped thug.

"Sure, it's me!" he answered, simulating perfectly the husky voice of Choppy, though he had heard it but briefly. "Who the hell did you think I was?"

The girl had vanished now. She was nowhere in sight.

Monk Gorman cursed. "What the devil you doin' out here, Choppy? Your orders was to wait in the house, so when that Phantom guy came —"

"Choppy was talkin' to the dame!" Gus put in.

"Sure, I was," Van returned. He knew he was on delicate, perilous ground now. For he still couldn't tell whether the girl had deliberately signaled these gunmen or not. "She stopped me and begun to talk. I'd come out-to see why the Phantom guy hadn't showed up," he said, with clever ambiguity.

"Okay, okay, forget it!" growled Monk Gorman. "So th' Phantom didn't fall for th' dame's gag, eh?"

"Maybe that blast really got him last night," Gus suggested.

"Nix!" Monk growled. "The boss said he's still alive."

Van's eyes narrowed imperceptibly. How could this "Boss" of theirs be sure that he was alive?

"Well, come on guys. No sense waitin' around-and cops might show." Monk Gorman gestured impatiently with his gun. "Jes' as well come, too, Choppy."

Choppy followed the rest obediently. He was grateful that they did not go back to the house. Either Gorman had forgotten or cared nothing about leaving Choppy's automatic rifle there.

The mob leader led the way hurriedly around a corner to the same dark sedan which had been used for Van's kidnaping the night before.

Once more the Phantom rode in that car, this time as a member of the gang, seated in the rear between Monk and Gus.

The ride proved a long one. The car worked eastward across the city as the night gathered. Again it rolled openly through traffic. Once it passed right by a police radio prowl-car —and Monk huddled back, gripping his gun. But the bluecoats did not suspect the sedan.

Van was silent-not risking any questions, lest he betray the fact he was an impostor. A grim hope sustained him as he played this perilous masquerade. If only it led him where he surmised it should.

The mists of another waterfront slowly engulfed the rolling car. The East River, this time. Up onto the ramp of the Queensborough Bridge. There was still no conversation, the gunmen evidently feeling tense while in traffic. The car followed the bridge traffic into Queens, and onto Vernon Boulevard.

Northward Tony now drove at a rapid clip through the deepening night. As the road grew more lonely, Monk Gorman sighed, leaned forward.

"We'll be plenty early tonight," he gruffed. "An' we ain't bringin' such good news. You sure you didn't see that Phantom guy, Choppy?"

"I tole you," retorted the man they thought was Choppy. "I was watchin' for him, all set to let him have it. Hell, you don't think I'd let that bird go if I got a chance to plug him, do ya?" Convincing underworld hatred of the Phantom threaded his tone.

"I guess you wouldn't." Gorman laughed evilly. "Not since the Boss fixed up that special medicine for crossers —the Ladle!"

As he pronounced those last words, Van saw the other thugs shudder perceptibly.

"The Ladle sure is a tough rap!" the broken-nosed Gus put in. "Maybe it wouldn't work in winter, but now —"

Tony gave a nervous laugh from the front seat:

"The Boss musta been in a hot country all right to think o' that one!"

Van made a pretense of joining their mingled awe and dread. What, he wondered, was this thing they called the Ladle? Why did they mention the "Boss" as having been in a hot country?

The gunmen fell silent again as lights and buildings loomed ahead. The sedan was rolling into Astoria. It passed on to the outskirts on to a road now where huge shed-like buildings, some of them having as many glass panes as greenhouses, reared in the night.

Motion picture studios! Here the big companies produced their small percentage of eastern-made pictures. Van's eyes narrowed in his disguised face. Gordon Drake owned some of those studios, he knew.

They passed the last of the line of sheds, rolled on a full mile more. And then, well-isolated from all the rest, another studio loomed. And here the car slowed.

This studio bore little resemblance to the modern structures they had passed. It looked small and old, deserted-with cracks in its many glass panes.

Obviously a relic of bygone days of the old silent movies which were thrown together hurriedly and cheaply, their casts composed of actors who were ashamed to be associated with the new show medium.

Even the grounds where it stood were deserted and isolated. The sedan turned into a side road and came to a stop before the dark building. In the gloom, Van saw other shadowy cars on the grounds.

"Okay, guys!" Gorman directed. "End of th' line."

The Phantom, his pulses throbbing, piled out of the car with the rest and followed Gorman to a boarded-up door. The leader gave a sharp rap, a timed signal and gruff challenge issued from within.

"Open up!" Monk growled.

The barrier opened. Past a shadowy, capped man who was evidently on guard, Monk led his companions. Through gloom, thence through another doorway, into the vast interior of the studio.

To Van's astonishment, there were lights here —a dim but ample illumination coming from bulbs strung on wires. His heart tightened with inner excitement. These lights were cleverly hidden despite the glass-paned building. For the glass was painted on the inside so it would be opaque. The paint looked fresh, recent.

Devilishly clever! From the outside this studio looked deserted, empty and dark. But inside it could teem with life.

The hum of many gruff, coarse voices filled the place. Standing or seated on packing boxes and other bits of equipment were a whole crowd of men, all of whom bore-in their manner, guise, or voice-the stamp of the underworld.

The Fang's gang! Assembled here, and members still coming in! Van recognized some of them. He saw the gash-mouthed man whose name was Pete, and whose shoulder was in a sling-Van had wounded him in that fight when he had posed as Eddie Collins. He saw others whom he recognized only by memory of rogue's gallery pictures.

Here in this old studio were gathered the co-ordinated mobsters of four former leaders who had been killed, their power usurped! The most powerful mob of desperadoes ever organized under one leadership! It was amazing.

They were all in attitudes of leisure. Some played cards, others smoked, others bent over a crap game. Van, still with Monk's crowd, walked into the midst of this devilish gathering, feeling like a man who has entered a den of beasts!

Inwardly, he prayed that his disguise was good enough to pass him by them all. That no one would suspect that he wasn't the real Choppy.

His eyes took in the strange surroundings. Piles of old sets in corners. Tarpaulin-covered shapes here and there on the floor. Part of the old equipment, presumably.

Monk swaggered through the gathering as voices greeted him.

"Okay, men, okay!" came his salutary reply. "We gotta wait here now, maybe some time. Meanwhile, let's see if we got everything ship-shape. Spike!"

A thug came forward.

"What'd you do with the bundle?" Monk asked, and Van saw the big man pale strangely.

"It's over there in the corner. I was afraid to get rid of it, Monk-until I got definite orders. Maybe somebody would find —"

"Okay. But hell, we don't want it around here. Well, leave it go."

Van had followed the speech closely, as well as the thug's pointing finger.

"Hey, Choppy-wanna come in?" one of the crap-shooters suddenly jerked up with the question.

"Naw," Van answered. Crap-shooting was something no two men did alike. He couldn't risk impersonating Choppy at rolling the dice. "Count me out tonight. I'm feelin' kinda low cause I didn't spot that Phantom guy."

"Well, can you beat that? First time Choppy ever dodged a crap game!" one of the others put in. And Van tensed. He must be careful, extremely careful.

Discreetly, he withdrew from the players. Moving unobtrusively, he threaded his way through the studio. He knew where he wanted to go, but he was taking his time getting there, making sure to attract no suspicion or attention.

Slowly, cautiously, he worked his way towards the corner of the studio to which the thug named Spike had pointed. As yet he saw nothing there but old refuse.

The atmosphere, he could feel now was getting tenser as the night deepened. There was a sense of expectancy among these thugs that made Van determined to stay here, to see this thing through. He had abandoned the idea of getting out while he still might manage it to call the police to surround the lair. For that would not catch the criminal he really sought.

Finally he drew close to that shadowy corner. He glanced around. No one looking this way. Monk had gone off to speak to others of the mob.

The Phantom moved swiftly, for a moment he was out of the role of Choppy, using his own lithe speed. The shadows of the corner engulfed him. His eyes darted around as he moved.

Suddenly his foot collided with something heavy, lumpy. He glanced down. There was a burlap bundle at his feet. It was not very large, yet Van felt a premonitory chill as he glanced at it. Something ugly and sinister about that bundle! He remembered Monk's paling face.

The Phantom stooped. His hands reached the burlap. He had to roll the bundle to get the covering off, so he gave a quick jerk. Then his blood went cold, as two bloody, gruesome shapes tumbled out of the wrapping.

A pair of human legs!

Legs hacked off above the knee, hideously amputated-with severed bone, bloody arteries and tendons showing raw and ghastly. But what filled the Phantom with a sense of horrified revulsion was the size of those legs.

They were small-spindly! The legs of a child!

For a moment all Van's conception of the case was thrown into a turmoil. Was this some new kind of crime of the devilish murderer who called himself the Fang? Was it possible that he had killed a helpless child?

Somewhere in the studio a bell clanged sharply.

It brought Van up rigid, made him whirl in alarm. Quick relief came as he saw that no eyes were turned in his direction. All were looking the other way, toward the other end of the studio.

Monk's voice rose then. "Get your places, everybody! Hurry! Choppy! Where the hell's Choppy?"

Chapter X
Klieg Lights

Just like that! Caught here at this moment, the Phantom knew suspicion would fasten upon him.

His mind raced. Then, deliberately, he raised his voice "Okay, okay, I'm comin'!"

But his voice did not seem to come from where he was hastily rewrapping the burlap around the gruesome, spindly legs. Instead, it seemed to come vaguely from the crowd of thugs. Ventriloquism was an art the Phantom had mastered along with all other arts of mimicry and disguise.

Quickly thrusting the gruesome bundle wrapped back into the shadows, he darted along the wall and came out in the center of the studio, presenting himself to Monk Gorman all in a breathless second.

"You stay by me," Monk ordered. "You gotta report on th' Phantom guy." As he spoke, others were busily removing the tarpaulin from the shapes Van had assumed to be old equipment. Black metal showed—a glimmer of glass. Then, a sudden hiss-and Van recoiled, his eyes suddenly blinded, dazzled.

A dozen super-powerful arc lights had suddenly gone on simultaneously. Kliegs! The modern, blazing lights of the movies! These were the shapes which the tarpaulins had hidden.

Their blinding flood blotted out the mild glow of other lights as though they had not been. Their heat permeated the studio almost like a blast.

The entire mob was thrown into vivid clearness, every face showing clear. Van felt trepidation about his make-up. He was glad he had spent some time putting on the disguise. For it must withstand that glare!

Monk seated himself on a packing case. Van followed suit. All others settled down facing the array of lights which, the Phantom saw, were grouped so that they came from one general direction-the opposite end of the studio. Blinking, the thugs must expose themselves to the full torture of the glare which was like a solid wall, beyond and behind which no human eye could possibly see.

As all voices ceased talking, and a hush fell over the assemblage, Van sensed a presence behind that wall of glaring light. An evil presence which intruded itself here in this strange studio hideout, making its horror felt even by the hardened crooks. Abruptly the silence was broken. A voice rang out from beyond the lights, a rasping, blighting voice: "This meeting is now in order! No one is to leave his place unless told to do so!"

Van listened carefully to the rasped tones, as his companions stiffened in mingled awe and dread. The Phantom could not identify the voice as any he had heard. He strained his eyes futilely to penetrate beyond the glare. Did he see a vague shape in that gloom beyond them? He could not tell-for the shape blurred into myriad dancing colors as his eyeballs ached from the sheer attempt.

"So far," the voice spoke again, "I have few complaints to make. You have proved yourself an obedient and efficient mob! Your former leaders must have trained you well! But they were small fry! You are working for a real Big Shot now! Already you have seen the returns! But that is what you, in your parlance, call chicken-feed! I have news for you tonight, good news!"

The men in the glaring light leaned forward with tense eagerness. Van's own eyes were narrowed now. His hand was close to the pocket where he had substituted Choppy's automatic pistol for his own.

He knew that the man who stood hidden behind that battery of light was indeed the criminal he sought, the brain behind this ghastly trail of death and robbery! But the criminal was well protected from any possible attack. Those lights made him an impossible target. He could see every face, every move, without being seen himself!

"I have news!" the voice rasped out. "Tomorrow the police of New York will see a robbery unparalleled! A robbery of millions-millions, which I shall share with you all! It is for this that I have prepared you, for this I have gathered you into one great mob!"

There was a tense, eager intake of breaths. Van's own lips tightened. A robbery! A climax to the crimes-tomorrow!

Monk suddenly rose now, spoke gruffly. "Listen, Boss! I'm in charge of it, ain't I? Have you changed your plans? Or are you gonna take care o' things at the office of that feller Drake?"

Even as Van pricked up his ears at the name, the voice of the master criminal snarled out with sudden menace that made Monk recoil. "That will do, Monk! I'll give you the proper orders at the right time."

Gordon Drake, the movie producer. And this was a studio! Why was the criminal so quick to suppress that name? Why had Monk mentioned it in connection with the robbery?

These questions raced through Van's mind while he listened. "Sometimes, Monk," the voice came like a purr now, "you are too impulsive! Perhaps Ricco, or one of those others, would have made a better lieutenant!"

"No, Boss!" Monk trembled. "Hell—I just sorta got excited, thinkin' of all that dough!"

"Very well. But be careful. Remember—*the Ladle* awaits bunglers as well as traitors!"

Again, this time from the criminal leader, came that peculiar name. And men shifted. Van saw several eyes glance upwards, towards the high ceiling. He saw nothing there but the cross-beams of a gallery and roof.

"I am impatient enough with you. You didn't get the Phantom tonight, did you?"

It was a statement rather than a question. The devilish Boss knew-somehow!

Monk spoke quickly, defensively. "He didn't show up, Boss. Only the dame showed. At least that's what Choppy says," he was quick to shift the blame. "He was talkin' to the dame when we come by to pick him up.

"Choppy!" Van's heart tightened as the criminal rasped out the name. "Step up front and let me have some words with you!"

The Phantom did not risk hesitation.

Rising, knowing that all eyes were on him, he strode forward before the gathering.

"Closer! I want to see you!"

Still Van dared not hesitate. He walked closer-until the array of lights met him, the heat of them engulfed him.

He felt sweat pop out beneath his make-up. Now he saw a dim, shadowy shape beyond the lights. But he could distinguish nothing. He could feel eyes probing him, scrutinizing him.

"Well, Choppy? Why did you talk to the girl?"

"It was like this, Boss," Van replied in the voice of Choppy. He told the same story he had told Gorman-that when the Phantom hadn't shown up he had gone out to look, the girl had accosted him, started talking to him, that he was trying to pump her when Monk startled her away.

"What did she say? Who did she think you were?" came the cross-examination from the gloom.

Van took the cue he read in that question. "She seemed to think I was the Phantom guy," he said, realizing how perilous was the implication of the words. "It was kinda dark, an'—"

"Oh—" There was a pause. Then, to Van's tense relief: "All right, Choppy." And Van turned to go from that hot glare which was searing his very flesh.

"Just a moment," the voice called him back, and he had to remain. "I want you to keep in mind, Choppy, and all the rest of you-that we must get the Phantom!" Hate threaded the rasping tones now. "He alone stands in my way, dares to cross my trail! He must be destroyed. Destroyed and—"

Abruptly, the voice broke off. Simultaneously, Van's heart stopped in its very beat! His every nerve flashed the frightful warning to his brain!

He felt it then! Something was oozing down his face, wet and sticky! Melting make-up!

The make-up of Choppy's features was changing, blurring and lengthening under the arch criminal's eyes. The Klieg lights! Van had not thought their heat was quite so strong! But they had done this deadly work!

There was a roar like that of a beast from the astounded leader.

The Phantom dropped to the floor, and began rolling to one side as a flash of flame leaped, just visible, from behind the lights. A flash of flame, and another!

He heard the bullets whine over his head, heard yells from the rest of the gang. He got out his own gun, whipped it around, fired two shots in the general direction whence those flashes had showed. But the uninterrupted roaring of that snarling voice told him he had missed.

"Grab him, you fools! He's an impostor! Hey, Rube!"

Van tried for another shot, this time in the direction of the voice, but, like a pack of sudden charging wolves, a score of thugs were upon him!

They, too, saw the running make-up now, and understood. For a moment Van thought they would tear him apart. Their feet kicked him so that his aching body doubled; their fists crashed to his sticky face, their revolvers swung like clubs at him. Disarmed, stunned, still blinded by the glare of lights, he could not resist capture.

He was yanked toward the front lights again. Monk's big paw, holding a handkerchief, was swabbing at his face. But the make-up, though smeared, was indelible enough to keep his real features covered-his only boon in this moment of trapped helplessness.

"So you thought to spy on us, did you?" the voice rasped out savagely. "I can guess who you are. You're the Phantom! What have you done to Choppy?"

Van neither denied nor affirmed anything. He was silent, inwardly fighting against a surge of despair. Those lights had betrayed him, and he had been neatly trapped!

"You won't talk? You'll regret that; you'll be raving for mercy!" came the savage voice. "Dawn is almost come, and the weather promises fair!" Van wondered at this poetic digression. "Whatever you may have learned here, Phantom, will never leave your lips!"

Van thought of what little he had learned. There was to be a robbery of tremendous magnitude. There was something connected with Gordon Drake's office. And there was-in a corner of this studio-the most jarring bizarre note in this whole mystery. A wrapped pair of childlike legs!

"Take him," the unseen criminal roared then, "to *the Ladle*!"

"Come on, guys!" Monk took up the command, in savage delight.

Chapter XI
A Trick with Mirrors

Helpless, the Phantom was dragged across the glare-lit floor of the studio, to one side, where there was a flight of ascending stairs.

The gangsters took him up to that gallery above. Then still further upwards, ascending a narrow steep stairs. The fresh air of outdoors suddenly smote the Phantom. He saw the sky above, the stars fading in the first grey flush of dawn.

They had taken him to the roof of the studio-to what seemed to be a huge pit in the otherwise slanted, glass-paned roof. At the edge of this sunken pit was a small, open-fronted shed. In it Van caught a momentary glimpse of gleaming levers.

He was lowered to this platform above the pit. Kept there by menacing guns and rough hands. He shifted his gaze to the pit itself.

Within the pit was a huge, globular affair. It had a peculiar sheen, reflecting off every trace of light, so that it seemed like an immense bowl of scintillating jewels, something like the mirror-set globes that twirled under the beam of a spot-light to reflect dots of light on a dance floor.

The Phantom knew at once what this was. That bowl was made of a collection of reflectors, the powerful concentrating reflectors used in motion picture making. It was a sun mirror of sinister and diabolical design.

Monk was talking to the broken-nosed Gus. "You'll stick here, Gus, an' take care o' this! You know how to move them levers! It's set now, by the Boss himself, for sunrise. You make the first change at six-thirty, an' every fifteen minutes after that. Here, I'm givin' you my watch-it keeps right time!"

Van, still twisting his head amid his captors, saw Monk handing over a large gold watch-saw Gus taking it.

At that moment, the Phantom noticed that his captors were momentarily relaxed.

Their eyes were on Monk and Gus.

A wave of grim desperation fired the Phantom's muscles with a sudden surge of strength. With a gritted oath, he leaped to his feet, his lithe body hurling upward in the very midst of his captors!

His feet crashed out before him like a ball of iron. It caught the heavy beefy face of the nearest thug and sent him sprawling. Before others could recover from their surprise, the Phantom hurled across the platform-against the broken-nosed Gus!

Gus snarled an oath. The rest, drawing their guns, dared not fire for fear of hitting their companions. Van's hand snaked down at Gus's wrists, one of which was still taped. He pushed Gus toward the shed while the latter wrestled furiously.

Even then the others closed in, raising revolver butts like vicious clubs. But the Phantom still fought with Gus in the faint, dim light of the open shed. His right hand was busy at Monk's watch while his left held Gus in a crushing head-lock.

A second more-give him a second more!

Myriad stars danced before his eyes as a gun-butt smashed against his skull. Hands, like talons, tore him away from the cursing, frightened Gus. The rain of blows left little consciousness in his body.

The next thing he knew, he was being taken down into that glittering, reflector-lined bowl. It swayed under gangster feet. In its very center was a metal shaft which rose vertically out of the base of the bowl like the stamen of a flower.

To this the Phantom was bound with steel wire! It seared through his clothes, through his very flesh.

He knew that he was trapped, was in the worst predicament that ever had overtaken him! Yet, even as the gangsters climbed out, leaving him here, there was a hope in his heart, even though it was a feeble hope.

"Okay, Gus! We gotta go," came Monk's voice. A moment later the big man's coarse face appeared, over the rim of the bowl. "So long, Phantom!" he gloated mockingly. "You'll be yellin' your head off soon enough! An' no one'll hear you! You may be a tough bird, but you'll jes' be a fried egg now. Sorry I can't wait to hear you sizzle."

The coarse face withdrew. There was a receding tramp of feet as the gang filed down from the roof. Only the broken-nosed Gus remained. He paced the platform above Van, glancing down now and then, first at the captive and then at his borrowed watch.

The Phantom had already begun to struggle carefully against his bonds. Thus far no bonds, or rope or wire, had ever been strong enough to hold him. He knew he could get out of these, but it would take time-too much time, he feared.

For now the sky was growing lighter. Dawn was on hand. And the wires were still searing deep into his flesh.

He heard sounds of motors-cars starting, gears shifting. He knew that the meeting was breaking up below. The mob was leaving to perpetrate that gigantic robbery while he remained here, helpless. The criminal leader, the murderer whom the police sought as Al Millett, the Fang, would be taking his secret departure while the Phantom was powerless to prevent him.

Going loose again, to commit more crimes! A murderer who had killed two men by brutally ripping out their sides, braining a third with a cudgel, leaving a fourth corpse with a broken crowbar in his skull and-Van thought of those childlike, spindly legs, and revulsion sickened him.

Gus swaggered above the rim of the Phantom's open-air prison, complete monarch of this domain by virtue of the departure of all the rest. He watched the sky eagerly.

The Phantom, struggling against the wire bonds at every opportunity, also watched the sky.

Slowly it began to redden in the East. The red turned to gold. The sun rose, bursting into slow but brilliant life. The bowl in which the Phantom stood bound glowed dazzlingly then in prismatic splendor. The rays of the sun hit the reflectors-and one and all, they awoke to life and magnified the rays, concentrated them upon the Phantom.

Even though the sun was as yet not in its full power, those intensified beams immediately seared through Van's clothes, began to warm, then blister his flesh! Sweat oozed down his face, down his body, in rivulets. *The Ladle* —diabolic invention of a devilish criminal-was beginning its fatal, ghastly work!

Van, with his knowledge of science had calculated that work on first glimpse of the device. It was simple-fiendishly simple. The bowl was so arranged that, by a mechanism, it could be turned with the moving sun at timed intervals, the levers in the shed motivating the turning. And each new angle would be calculated to cause the sunlight gathered by its concave-mirror walls to focus on the Phantom's bound body!

Van Loan understood now why the crooks had mentioned the likelihood of the Boss having come from a "hot country." They were right; he had come from Hell.

Even now the blinding, concentrated heat was growing. It was eddying upon the Phantom in waves. His eyes were unable to meet it, his flesh seemed to coil and wither. His sweat was drying now. And the wires that still held him were also growing unbearably hot!

To yell was futile-else he would not have been left ungagged. He must conserve his strength; he must keep cool. He had used his most consummate skill and science while wrestling with Gus. Had he miscalculated?

"Well, Phantom? How's the weather down there now?" The mocking tones of Gus floated down to him. Through his already heat-swollen eyes he saw the broken-nosed thug through a red haze. "At six-thirty I'll give you a little swing."

The Phantom worked desperately at his bonds. With the heat blaze that enveloped him growing ever hotter, he could not long withstand it. Death would be a matter of perhaps a half hour of such exposure —a long half-hour of torture, of blistering flesh, of blinded eyes! For the sun was shining at him through so many magnifying glasses; the bowl was hot as blazing fire.

He struggled coolly, systematically—knowing well that it would take him more than thirty minutes to get out of this wire. As it was, he knew he could not retain consciousness for many more minutes. His very stoicism was rebelling against the agony of the heat which had not yet begun to do its real damage.

Tropical death in Astoria! It seemed an ironical joke —a crazy paradox. Yet, it was coming if he had made an error. He gritted his teeth. He would know shortly, at least. And then, when he really felt his face beginning to blister, Gus's voice chortled again.

"Six-thirty —an' Monk's watch is always right!"

Gus's footsteps banged on the wooden platform beyond the rim. He went into the shed to the levers. There came a sound of meshing cogs, the hum of electricity. *The Ladle* began moving like a huge swing. And at that moment Van clung to the one hope that sustained him.

He waited breathlessly for the effect of the moving bowl. Timed properly, it would only bring the sun's shifting rays hotter upon him. But improperly timed, it would be out of focus.

His heart soared! The blaze of light that was meant to destroy him shifted just a little to one side of his bound body, as the wabbling bowl went still. Those rays were no longer directly upon him, though the bowl itself was still a fiery furnace.

Would Gus see this? Would his coarse faculties be shrewd enough to comprehend the truth? This had been the whole purpose of that desperate scuffle with Gus. Knowing he could not make any real break at that moment for liberty, he had managed to do the one thing that was now reprieving him temporarily.

He had managed deftly, while keeping Gus's attention distracted by the struggle, to reset Monk's watch-setting it forward by about eight minutes. Eight minutes, enough to upset this device which was as mathematical as a moving sundial. Gus had not been told what time the sun began its work. He had been told only to start working the lever at six-thirty and make an adjustment every fifteen minutes thereafter.

Hence the sun was now thrown off. Its blazing concentration point, unless Gus suspected, would stay where it was, to one side of the Phantom. And Van, no longer in the direct glare, began to recover his strength; his remarkable stamina quickly generating new energy.

Gus's head appeared again above the rim. He peered down, blinking. The brilliant reflectors defied detection of the actual concentration point.

Lest he look closer, Van now did the thing which his stoicism had repressed when he was in real agony. He opened his dry mouth, began to groan, to yell, to shout in cries of pain.

A cruel, mocking laugh rose above him. "Boy, oh boy, wish the gang was here!" Gus chortled. "They'd like this-seein' how the Phantom can't really take it after all! How he's just as human as the rest of us! Cripes! I wish I had a pair o' smoked glasses."

He turned away, chortling.

Van again worked at the wires, worked until another fifteen minutes had passed. Which he knew when again the bowl tilted and the motor hummed. Once more the sun-glare of concentration remained fixed to one side of his body.

And then one arm came wresting out of the wires. The wrist caught, the wire cutting into it excruciatingly. Van let the pain of it out in another deliberate yell. He twisted the wrist, deftly, carefully at the same time.

It came free. One arm free was all the Phantom needed. The rest was a matter of seconds.

The wires slid jerkily off his lithe body. He moved from the shaft, moved to the sloping side of the bowl just beneath the platform. When he tried to touch it, the heat of the mirrors seared his hands. He tore some of his own borrowed clothing off to use as protection.

There was purchase in the interstices between the reflectors, and he began to climb, the heat beating against his body. A little further now-almost to the rim —

A yell of enraged alarm greeted him. Gus, turning on the platform, had seen! With a snarl the thug leaped forward, gun whipping out. At the same instant, the Phantom's body literally catapulted over the rim, over and forward!

Leaping with all his strength, Van Loan caught the thug's gun arm as the frenzied man was taking aim! Instantly the two were struggling in a fierce conflict on the platform! Struggling against the very rail of the platform, beyond which the high studio roof inclined with its opaque panes of glass.

Gus, who was powerfully built, was fighting like a frightened beast ... realizing he was up against the scourge of the underworld, a man he had twice seen make miraculous escapes from certain death. Snarling, he pushed Van with his whole body against the wooden rail.

It splintered, opening a gap. The Phantom's feet pulled him up as he swayed perilously. Then, both his hands caught the thug who was lurching against him. The thing he next did was instinctive.

A jiu jitsu hold, and Gus, heavy though he was, went flying through the air over the Phantom's head. Screaming, the thug landed on the slanted glass roof. The panes shattered, but the metal framework held. Gus fell forward from the impetus, his body rolling, rolling. Grim-eyed, Van saw it reach the roof's edge. Saw it topple off and go hurtling down through fully sixty feet of space, to the stone paving below. There was a ghastly thud. The body, a tiny heap down there, lay still The Phantom swore grimly. Gus, alive, might have told him where that big robbery was to take place. But again he had had no chance to take one of this desperate mob alive.

He walked tiredly to the roof entrance, into the studio, downward through its interior.

The place was empty. Even that burlap-wrapped bundle-and all other evidence was gone. The only thing left to do was to find where the big robbery was to be, and to prevent it if possible.

He stood, swaying, exhausted and dizzied from his ghastly experience. For a moment he felt too tired to go on-tired enough to drop right here. But then, remembering Monk Gorman's reference to Gordon Drake, his body straightened; a purposeful gleam leaped once more into his sun-dazzled eyes. He sprinted from the building.

Chapter XII
The Armored Truck Job

Morning activity to the average New Yorker, seemed the same as it did any other sunny morning-the usual bustle of traffic and scurrying workers.

But actually there was a difference. All over the city police patrols had been doubled. Extra prowl-cars were sweeping through every precinct. Squads of detectives, men who usually waited at station houses for their calls, were out on the streets, keen-eyed and alert.

For the police had received a tip from that Nemesis of Crime, the Phantom. Somewhere a big robbery was about to break! And, while they scoured the streets, Richard Curtis Van Loan himself stood, grim and expectant, in a closet in the empty office of Gordon Drake, motion picture producer.

Again the Phantom was masked, the domino covering the features of a slightly vacant-faced young Englishman in tweeds. He had slipped into this towering office building before it had opened. His pliable bit of wire had picked the lock of Gordon Drake's office. He was waiting for that which was supposed to break at Drake's office.

Van had come to New York from the abandoned studio in Astoria in a car. He had stopped off at his own penthouse apartment on Park Avenue for a shower, shave, breakfast, and fresh change of clothes. He was little the worse for his grueling experience-though his face was red with sunburn, under his make-up.

At his apartment, Van had phoned Inspector Gregg, and then called the New York Academy of Medicine, which had someone on duty night and day. He had requested a service of them, a service that required them to canvass, by their own swift means of communication, doctors throughout an entire nation!

"If you get any answers-kindly hold them for me," Van had finished. He had identified himself as the Phantom in that call, explaining that the evidence was vital to his case.

From Inspector Gregg he had learned of the progress of the case. The police were still investigating the mysterious Count Karnov. They were still rounding up any persons remotely resembling the Fang's description. Bernard J. Andrews was still missing. Also, Queen Stella.

Van had taken these facts, then given his instructions to the police.

Now, cramped in the closet of Drake's sumptuous office, he waited patiently.

Presently, as the morning sun slanted wider through the office windows, Van heard a key in the lock. He pulled the closet door to a chink, through which he could still command a view.

The frosted-glass door opened. Gordon Drake, the heavy-set movie producer, strode in alone. He took off his cap stiffly, but left on his cape-like topcoat.

He glanced about the office. Then, scowling, he began to pace back and forth as if waiting. Van remained motionless in the closet.

Came a knock on the door. "Come," growled Drake, as though he expected it.

Into the room strode two more of the men involved in the Fang case, men Van recognized as Drake pronounced their names.

"Hello, Corbin-good morning, Meade!"

Paul Corbin, slender and effeminate night-club owner. Kenneth Meade, the eccentric restaurateur who wore a long, tight buttoned coat and articulated with difficulty.

Somehow, seeing the three of them together, Van sensed again that queer feeling all the men involved gave everybody-something strange, intangible, they had in common.

The three stood looking at each other. It was Corbin who spoke. The little man seemed agitated.

"Drake, are you going to give your consent to this foolish plan!" he asked in his high voice.

Drake shrugged. "It's out of my hands," came his reply. "I don't care a hoot, to tell you the truth."

Meade shifted his heavy-coated frame. "I told Corbin he is on the wrong track," he said in a hard labored voice.

"All right!" Corbin shrilled. He waved an angry hand at them. "You're going to regret this, both of you. Mark my words!" Despite its shrillness, there was menace in his tones. "You all think you're clever-but you're fools, see! Fools!"

He whirled angrily, started for the door.

"Where are you going?" Drake demanded. "What are you up to now, Corbin?"

Carbon's eyes blazed with a light that seemed almost fanatical to the watching Phantom.

"I'm going out to prove," he said, as if too impulsive to weigh his words, "that the police can still be fools, as well as you! That vast amount of money —"

He broke off and stalked through the door. Meade started uncertainly after him.

"Sit down, Meade," Drake said dryly. "There's really nothing we can do now. The Gargoyles must trust each other. Corbin can do nothing."

The closet door swung open, revealing a masked man with leveled automatic.

"But there's a great deal that I can do," Van's voice clipped, cold as the steel of his own Colt automatic. "Do not move, gentlemen, if you value your lives!"

Drake and Meade recoiled, violently startled.

"The Phantom!" exclaimed Drake, face paling.

"Right," snapped Van Loan. "I'll talk with you men later. Just now I've an engagement with Mr. Corbin. Remain quietly here, if you value your lives."

He heard an elevator door closing even then. Corbin going down! Leaving the two speechless and immobile, he darted out of the office and sprinted for the elevator bank. He was not followed.

As he reached the elevator doors, pressing the down button, the Phantom took off his mask. To his satisfaction, an express elevator stopped for him in the next instant.

"Go straight down, buddy," he directed the operator.

"But I —" the capped man's protests ceased at the sight of the bill extended towards him. The elevator didn't even make its express stops.

As it reached the main floor, its doors sliding open, Van saw that the other elevator which had preceded it more slowly was just coming to a stop. The slender figure of Corbin, hatless, walked hurriedly through the foyer and out the main glass doors. Behind him walked a pleasant looking but vacant-faced Englishman.

Van Loan saw Corbin climb into a small, expensive roadster. The motor started with a hasty grind of the self-starter. The car slid from the curb, quickly gathered speed as it headed across town.

Van hurried down the pavement, climbed into the coupe which he had left parked there. It was a coupe he had borrowed from the Police Department-one with special equipment with which the police were recently experimenting.

The Phantom's eyes flashed through the windshield even as he got the coupe going. Corbin's car was shrinking across the next intersection. Van stepped on the gas, maneuvered the coupe deftly through traffic, and when he was not far behind the roadster, he settled down grimly to the trail.

Across town his quarry led him, then onto Broadway, headed down-town. Corbin drove faster now, almost recklessly in the morning traffic. Once he passed a red light. Van passed it, too.

Broadway narrowed as the two cars finally reached its lower extremities, coming into the financial district with its tall skyscrapers and narrow, canyon-like streets. The roadster swung east, went onto Broad Street. It turned south again. Then, so suddenly that Van scarcely had time to follow suit, the roadster skidded to an abrupt stop.

It had stopped almost opposite a square stone building on the corner —a prominent bank which had its own truck entrance.

Out of that entrance now, a green-turreted armored truck was rolling, obviously leaving the bank on some errand. The truck turned onto Broad Street.

Van was still pressing down his own brake pedal, eyes on Corbin's roadster which had stopped almost in front of the truck. And now, astonishingly, Corbin's slender figure leaned out of its open door. Corbin was waving at the armored truck-commanding it to stop.

In the next instant, even as a chill premonition flashed through Van, several things happened at once, all with the breathless rapidity of a speeded-up motion picture.

The armored truck slowed momentarily. Its green turret swung warningly. Two sedans, a Buick and a Cadillac, suddenly curved clear across the street from the other side, their gears meshing. From two angles they converged towards the armored truck, which Corbin's car had already partially blocked.

The Phantom's foot left the brake pedal, going to the accelerator. His hand was on the gear-shift, his eyes tense and grim. He sent the coupe hurtling forward.

Above his engine he heard a spurt of fire. It came from the turret of the armored truck. A repeating rifle-shooting warningly.

The Cadillac sedan suddenly swung straight in then, to one side of the green truck. Van gave a cry. He saw something dark and heavy come hurtling out of the Cadillac's rear window, arc through the air and —A most deafening explosion shattered the morning air! A great blinding sheet of flame which quickly turned into smoke blotted out the entire armored truck from view.

The Phantom felt his coupe shiver with that reverberating concussion which shook his very teeth. The shatter-proof windshield in front of him became a mass of spider-webs. He heard screams as the explosion died-saw people on the pavement who had been hurled several feet, some of them badly hurt.

He was still driving the shaken coupe towards the scene. The billowing smoke was just dissipating. He caught a glimpse of the armored truck-and his heart chilled. The heavy vehicle was overturned, its wheels kicking around like some wounded animal's. Its armor plate was dented, broken.

Slouch-hatted figures were leaping upon it like human vultures. Van saw a big, slicker-clad form amid them. Monk Gorman! He saw them jerking open the shattered door of the armored truck.

As he continued to drive towards the scene, eyes grim as death, his hand moved to the dashboard of his coupe where there was an unusual array of dials. He turned a switch. He yanked out a microphone hanging by its wire to the dash. Driving with one hand, he spoke into the microphone in crisp tones: "Calling all cars —1st Division!" he bit out. "All cars-Signal 30! Signal 30! Armored car hold-up in progress at Broad Street and Fourth Street. Signal 30!"

He knew that his every word went through the powerful transmission set in this car. Tuned to the short-wavelength of every prowl-car in the city, it went out through the ether from the antenna atop Van's coupe. For this car was one of the only two cars in the Department that could send out radio calls even as the Voice at Headquarters sent them out.

Now the Phantom was at the scene. He saw the slouch-hatted mobsters snatching bags and packages out of the armored truck, working with speed and efficiency. In mere seconds they had evidently taken their loot-were scurrying back to the two waiting sedans, ignoring the damaged roadster of Corbin and the coupe of Van Loan.

The Cadillac started in the next instant. It swung away, bearing off its part of the loot.

The Phantom dropped the microphone, took the wheel in both hands, his lips a tight line of fierce purpose. He sent the little coupe careening around the scene in a spurt of speed to head them off-at least delay them!

The Cadillac was gathering speed. The Phantom pushed his accelerator to the floorboard. The coupe arced past the Cadillac, then diagonaled in on the big, fleeing car.

A tommy gun began its snarling chatter. Van heard bullets pelt like hail against the coupe's sides. One slug whined through the open window past his face. He glanced to one side and back-saw Monk's coarse features in the rear open window of the Cadillac behind the gibbering tommy.

The Cadillac, heavier and larger than the coupe, tried to threaten it out of the way with heavy iron fenders. Van swerved out. The Cadillac started to pass him. He saw it would get away.

He pulled his wheel hard around, his lithe body bracing simultaneously as he floor-boarded his accelerator. Like a startled deer, the coupe leaped into the side of the heavy Cadillac at an angle he thought should enable it to take the crash without completely telescoping.

There was a frightful impact of metal against metal. The coupe shivered, shaking every bone in the Phantom's body. Water spurted from the radiator, steamily. Then, with a shrieking of tortured metal, the coupe was dragged sideways. The Cadillac, locked by its running board with the coupe's fenders, tried desperately to pull the lighter car with it.

Monk's face leaned out-murderous, livid, Van ducked as he saw the tommy swinging to hose down the police car. Then, even as he thought the tommy would blast his stanch little coupe to ribbons, he saw Monk and the others start to abandon the Cadillac like frightened rats.

Only then did he hear the scream of sirens, scores of sirens, filling the already noise-shattered street. Police cars! Green coupes! Hurtling dark cruisers! Coming from two directions, turning in from every side street! Blockading the whole vicinity!

The Phantom's radio call had brought a response. Those cars had been waiting for just such a signal. "Signal 30 —come quickly with drawn guns!"

Van leaped out of his wrecked, tangled coupe. The street was full of fresh sounds of gunfire now. Police positives roared. Smoke curled insidiously in the sun. Flame flashed. And thugs from both bandit cars were going down, riddled bodies hurling, bloody, to the street.

It was over by the time the Phantom limped out of his wreck. Grim-jawed cops were sheathing their guns. Others were trying to gather the bundles of currency, the bags, which were strewn amid the dead and in the two sedans. And other policemen began pulling out what was left of the men of the armored truck crew. Two had apparently died from the explosion; a third had been riddled by the gangsters. The fourth and fifth were badly maimed and unconscious.

* * *

"Well, we got a good part of the mob, anyway-even if Monk Gorman and two other of his men escaped!"

Five minutes later, in the ornate office of the bank, Inspector Gregg, who had also answered the radio call, spoke these words as he mopped his placid but heavy face with a handkerchief. "And from the looks of it, Phantom, you enabled us to save a large portion of the swag! How much did you say, Mister?"

This to the shaken, grey-haired president of the bank who was stacking piles of currency and bonds, some of them stained with blood, on his desk.

"Over two million dollars here." He announced the staggering sum, then shook his head. "The audacity of those thieves! It's lucky the money was saved. Certainly the bonding company would think there was something queer about the truck being robbed at our very doors! They'd say we didn't give it proper protection-or that there was some sort of inside work."

The Phantom having identified himself in his present disguise to the chief of detectives, glanced across the office. In a chair, attended by two policemen, sat Paul Corbin. The man's face was cut, and he seemed dazed, but he had refused ambulance attention.

"You say the original sum was almost three million," the Phantom then spoke to the bank president. "Isn't it unusual to send out such a sum? And on the face of it, don't you think you should tell us who authorized it, and where it was to go?"

The bank president hesitated. Then he made a gesture as if laying cards on the table. "The securities and money belonged to the Star Corporation," he announced. "They were being shipped to one of its authorized officers over in Brooklyn."

Van's eyes narrowed. The Star Corporation! The corporation which owned the building of the Gargoyle Club! He turned to the dazed Corbin.

"Well, Corbin, do you feel ready yet to offer an explanation?" he asked crisply.

"Explanation?" Corbin echoed. "What for? What have I done?"

"Why did you rush down here, and wave that armored truck to stop?"

The inspector, to whom this was news, turned with an exclamation. "What's that? He stopped the truck?"

Corbin was on his feet then, shakily.

"Yes —I tried to stop this fool move! And I'll tell you why!" he cried, a wild note in his voice. "Some of that money, a good part of it, belongs to *me!* And I didn't want it taken out of the vaults here! The others wouldn't listen to me. I told them it was dangerous. I told them that Gifford was making a stupid, blundering move —"

"Gifford?" the inspector echoed, while Van showed no surprise, remembering that John Gifford, amusement park owner, was president of the Star Corporation.

"Yes, Gifford! He sent the order. He was going to store our securities in his new big vault at Coney Island. The others refused to interfere! They said Gifford had the best business brain-if he made a move like this he must know it was the only move!"

Van turned with tacit inquiry to the bank president. Slowly that official nodded. "Yes, the order was authorized by John Gifford," he said.

The inspector's brow screwed into deep lines. "That's funny. Gifford ordering the movement of a lot of dough when he knows this Al Millett is on the loose with his gang, plundering and robbing all the men involved!"

The Phantom nodded. "I think," he suggested, "that it might pay to have an interview with Mr. Gifford about now."

Chapter XIII
The Fang Claims Another Victim

Driving rapidly, the Phantom sat beside the inspector in the latter's shield-fronted limousine a few minutes later as they headed into Brooklyn, and onto the highway to Coney Island to interview Gifford.

They had allowed Paul Corbin, still shaken and dazed, to go home from the bank, intending to grill him plenty a bit later.

With screaming siren giving it a clear road, the inspector's car made the trip to Coney Island in record time. Nevertheless it was well past noon when the maze of Ferris wheels, scenic railway tracks, carousels, and other amusement machines in which millions found thrills and pleasure loomed before the inspector's car, then engulfed it on Surf Avenue.

Gifford's Park was doing only a modest business now, at the tail end of the season. Most of the attractions were closed, although others were just opening up. Uniformed attendants guided the inspector's car to a small, but massive concrete building-Gifford's new offices and vault.

Getting out of the limousine, the Phantom and the inspector strode in. A man was pacing the office floor-agitated, worried looking. It was not Gifford! It was Carl Fenwick.

The clerical looking producer looked up with startled eyes which widened quickly at sight of Van Loan's innocuous face.

"Police?" he breathed. "Here?"

"Yes. What brought you out here, Mr. Fenwick?" Van asked casually.

"Gifford phoned for me to come!" Fenwick answered. "Said he had some news to tell me. I'm waiting for him now."

"He isn't here?" the inspector demanded.

"He was here. Just said 'hello' to me, then bolted out in a hurry-said he had to attend to something, and for me to wait."

The Phantom's eyes were suddenly tense. "When was that?"

"About three minutes ago, perhaps even less."

The inspector scowled. "That was just about the time we were coming into the Park! Wonder if he got word we were here?"

The Phantom, who had already considered that possibility, hurried to the door, out onto the Park grounds. The tension was still in his eyes; a strange apprehension was tightening around his heart.

He crisped a question at a special Park policeman standing on the pavement. The latter replied, "Yes, I saw Mr. Gifford. He went over that way-toward the Leap-for-Life."

He pointed toward the maze of spiraling tracks of the big rocket railway designed by the owner. It had evidently just started running. Two streamlined cars, half-filled with patrons, were beginning the ascent on one side, being dragged by the moving cable up the incline.

The Phantom quickened his fast stride, the somewhat confused inspector at his heels. They hurried toward the gigantic, futuristic railway.

At that instant, above the faint clatter of the climbing cars, there sounded a hoarse cry! A cry of terror —a feeble but blood-curdling sound drifting from far above!

Galvanized by the sound, the Phantom catapulted forward, his eyes darting upwards. Through the lattice-like, open trackwork, just in the middle of the arc of the first long and steepest hill of the railway, he glimpsed a vague, dark bulk!

The Phantom jerked his head back, crisped out with fierce haste, "Get them to turn off the power! Hurry, before those cars reach the top of the hill!"

He did not wait to see his command carried out. Never before had he moved with more lightning rapidity. He leaped for a ladder-one of the many ascending the framework of the tracks. The Phantom scrambled up like a monkey.

In seconds he was nearing the top. Simultaneously, his ears told him the cable had stopped moving. The power had been shut off. But then-His heart went chill!

On top of the long steep incline, he heard a rumble, a clattering rumble which grew rapidly louder. One of those cars had reached the hill crest before the power had been turned off. It was going over that crest! Like a rocket, it was coasting down the hill, hurtling earthward with its passengers!

The Phantom spurred his body up with a terrific lunge, climbed over the open track-work. He glanced up the converging rails of the steep ascent, saw the car coming down now, swaying and rocking with its roaring speed!

In the center of the tracks before him writhing weakly, huddled the corpulent figure of John Gifford.

He was not bound, seeming merely to have been stunned, and thus unable to move.

"Gifford!" Van yelled above the roaring, downcoming rocket car. "Gifford!"

Gifford raised his head, stirring a little clumsily, but remaining on the track. The Phantom got his footing on a tie, caught hold of a metal strut, and leaned out over the track as he saw the car growing huge-coming on like a juggernaut! A juggernaut that threatened to mangle and kill both Gifford and him-and perhaps wreck and kill its own passengers as well!

He swooped down in that instant, got the man by the collar and heaved. Despite his corpulent appearance, Gifford proved such a surprisingly light burden, that Van nearly jerked him over the outside of the track-edge.

He recovered his balance and held Gifford against the framework just as the massive car whizzed by like a rocket.

Then, hands of park workers who had come up the ladder reached out. They got Gifford down and the Phantom lowered himself over the edge.

One of his hands was skinned where the rushing car had lightly touched it.

Fenwick and the inspector were on hand below when the dazed Gifford was brought down. He stood, shaken and pale, looking confusedly at the masked Phantom.

"You-you saved my life, sir," he gasped weakly. "I couldn't move!" Stark terror was growing in his eyes. "I was called out by phone-told there was some trouble under the scenic track. I went there-and never knew what hit me! The next thing I knew I was on the track and the car was coming down."

The inspector, listening, dispatched policemen who had arrived at the scene to search the grounds. "It's the Fang again or I miss my guess!" he cursed. "Lord, will he never end this reign of terror?"

Fenwick, standing by white-faced, blurted out, "If only *you* would end it! Gifford, why wouldn't you and the others —"

Gifford jerked up his head fiercely. "No! Drake was right. I wanted to see you about that, Fenwick!" He seemed now to have made an almost remarkable recovery; his voice was strong now-the dominant voice of a hard-fisted, successful business man. "I took certain measures to protect our interests."

"If you mean that you ordered three million dollars shipped to you in an armored car," Van put in sharply, "those measures were not sufficient. We've just come from the attempted hijacking of that fortune!"

"What?" Both Gifford and Fenwick stared with bulging, horrified eyes, chorusing the exclamation in unison.

Then Fenwick almost screamed, "You ordered out that truck! Damn you, Gifford, you had no right —"

"Wait!" Gifford put in. His voice shook now with a horror that seemed greater than he had shown before. "I didn't give such an order!" he cried. "I was considering it-but I didn't give it! That's what I wanted to talk about. I was merely going to have the bank put an extra guard on the money-God! *Someone forged my name to that order!* No wonder they tried to kill me! To cover up —"

The inspector spoke grimly. "This Al Millett did go in for some forging," he said slowly. "I wonder —"

The Phantom, too, was wondering. There was something strangely pat about Gifford's alibi. At the same time, Van felt a sense as of anticlimax. As if, despite the hectic rescue he had just made, his nerves had been braced for something that hadn't happened, yet which he felt was still in the air.

He turned to Gifford, started to frame more questions. At that instant an attendant came running from the concrete office building.

"Inspector! Call from your Headquarters! Urgent!"

The inspector's heavy frame charged across the ground. The Phantom, nerves going tense again, followed.

A waiting hand-set phone was ready for the inspector. He scooped it up. "Inspector Gregg talking. What?" An invisible spring seemed to straighten his whole body. "Okay-okay —"

He slammed down the instrument, whirled to the Phantom, who knew even before the inspector spoke that the climax he had missed had come after all.

Nevertheless, the inspector's shaken voice rang out like a knell.

"Kenneth Meade has just been murdered!" he announced. "Let's go!"

Leaving Fenwick and Gifford at the amusement park, guarded by uniformed police, the Phantom and Inspector Gregg sped back to Manhattan. The inspector's car rolled up Seventh Avenue and came to a stop before a huge restaurant facade-Milady's Salon.

Prowl-cars, cruisers, and riot squad trucks were already at the scene. The police were herding back a crushing mob-roping them off. The restaurant was empty of patrons-it functioned only at night.

The inspector and the Phantom strode through gaps in the saluting bluecoats, entered the premises. They found men with cameras already at work, the Homicide Squad busy at the scene.

Threading their way through tables piled with napkins but unset, they came to a spot at one end of the floor where the knot of detectives was thickest, and where the stocky Medical Examiner was at work.

Kenneth Meade, restaurateur, was sprawled with arms and legs rigidly outstretched. He lay on his back, but his body had a half-doubled aspect. His face was contorted in a grimace of agony, the lips horribly bluish, the sightless eyes protruding from their sockets as if they must pop out.

The clothes of the dead man had been ripped from his upper torso, exposing his neck and chest nakedly. In the naked flesh, in the lower part of the neck, just under his Adam's apple, was a hideous gash —a deep cut from which blood still slowly oozed.

"What is it, Doc?" the inspector demanded hoarsely. "Was he stabbed in the neck?"

The doctor rose slowly. If ever a man looked shaken, thrown entirely out of his professional equilibrium, this stocky city medical examiner did. "Yes, he was stabbed, but that didn't kill him," he said in a small, dazed voice. "The gash you see missed the trachea and went directly into the *esophagus* —the canal which takes food to the stomach. A man will live with such a wound."

"Then what —?" the inspector demanded, bewildered. The Phantom said nothing as he noted the rigid aspect of the corpse.

"Poison!" the doctor pronounced then, his voice shaking. "Bichloride of mercury, from the symptoms. Poison which was fed to Meade through that gash in his esophagus-which carried it to his stomach!" He shook his head. "This is a death unparalleled in all my career as a doctor. Evidently the criminal decided he wanted to poison Meade-but why he put it through a gash in the esophagus instead of through the mouth, I can't understand."

Sickened, the inspector turned away from the gruesome sight. Turned away only to stare with fresh horror at the tiny but familiar object a homicide officer now held out to him on a handkerchief.

"Found this next to the body, inspector," he said.

The inspector's eyes blazed. "I thought so! The Fang again! The same saber-tooth guy! At least he couldn't have been at Coney Island this afternoon to put Gifford on the track! He's making a laughing stock of us! With our whole department after him, he still goes right on, killing, plundering-He's getting in my hair."

"I wouldn't be too sure of that, inspector," observed Van Loan thoughtfully. "Meade could have been wounded, poisoned, and left unconscious to die slowly while the Fang went out to do other devilment. Just because Meade has just died doesn't mean the crime was just committed. It could have happened any time since I left him in Drake's office this morning."

A sudden commotion interrupted the conversation. Into the restaurant came a group of plainclothes men, dragging a struggling figure in their midst.

Van's eyes went sharp. The figure was the bearded, saturnine Count Karnov, the mysterious foreigner who had been at the Palladium the other night!

"We found this bird sneakin' around outside!" one of the detectives said. "And I think we found something on him that might answer a lot of questions!"

Karnov scowled, still struggling silently. The detective handed a paper to the inspector. "This was in his pocket, sir! Take a look. And get ready for a shock!"

The Phantom was at the inspector's shoulder as the latter lifted the paper. It was torn. There was a hasty scrawl in ink across it.

Even the Phantom gasped as he read it.

—so I've decided to send you a last warning.
—Al.

"Did you write this?" the inspector's voice was sharp as a knife as he faced the Count belligerently.

Karnov's dark eyes glowered.

"I refuse to answer any questions," he said in his flawless English.

"Oh, you do?" the inspector's hulk looked ominously menacing. "Well, do you deny that you're Al Millett?"

At the mention of that name, Karnov gave a perceptible start. He smiled then—a nasty, venomous smile. "You'll have a difficult time proving that, inspector." But there was desperation in his eyes.

The Phantom, with his keen knowledge of psychology, could see that the man wanted to get away quickly. Those glowering eyes were looking about furtively, like those of a trapped animal who would take the first possible loophole of escape.

"I'd like to really see the face you've got under that beard!" the inspector grated now. "Wait until we get you down to Headquarters! I think we'll have the end of these crimes!"

Karnov wet his lips, but was still silent. Van's mind was racing now. He moved across the floor. In the center of the big restaurant stood an immense porcelain vase, its top, about three feet above the floor, gaped dark and empty.

Van looked at the vase. It signified more than a vase to him. It was here for a purpose, a common thing in prominent European restaurants.

The Phantom picked up a napkin idly from a table. "I think I'd like to ask Count Karnov a few questions," he smiled. "Bring him here, please."

The detectives pushed the prisoner, whose eyes now were fixed darkly on the Phantom, across the floor. They stood back, a confident circle surrounding the man.

Van, standing at the vase, spoke carefully. "You're in a pretty tough spot, Karnov, as we say in police parlance." He dropped the napkin idly into the vase. It disappeared completely in the gaping interior. "The evidence is stacked pretty strongly against you. The police have ways of making men talk, when they get them down to Headquarters. So —"

A sudden, animal-like cry of desperation burst from Count Karnov's lips. He dived head first into the huge vase. So swiftly did he move that his guards were taken unawares. The inspector and others rushed to the vase while Van Loan stood quietly by.

"Come out of there, Karnov," rapped Gregg. "You fool, what good will that move do you?"

He broke off, face going bewildered, eyes filling with uncanny incredulity as he reached into the depths of the vase. "Why, he's gone! He's not in there at all! There's no bottom to this damned thing!"

The Phantom smiled and spoke. "I wanted him to think he was escaping, inspector. You carry on here. I'll find him all right." He whirled and hurried out of the premises. Out on the street Van slipped past the police-lined front of the restaurant, around the corner on which it stood, to the side of it. He was not surprised to glimpse a furtive figure crawling from a cellar exit of the building. The disheveled but desperate figure of Count Karnov!

No police were watching this side of the restaurant at the moment. When Karnov's eyes darted around furtively, the Phantom's lithe shape quickly flattened against the building. Count Karnov turned, dashed the opposite way up the block, running on legs obviously guided by sheer desperation.

The Phantom, slipping out, followed him.

On Sixth Avenue, Karnov hailed a taxi, leaped into it, slamming the door. The cab turned around, sped uptown. The Phantom hailed another taxi. He displayed a bill to the driver.

"Follow that cab!" he commanded. "But keep well behind it."

Chapter XIV
Trapped in the Penthouse

Affably the cabby nodded. Like most cabbies, he knew that kind of work. The trail did not prove difficult to follow, though it was a devious one.

It led uptown, through the oasis-like green of Central Park, out through Seventy-Second, thence over to West End Avenue.

The afternoon was already lengthening into dusk when Karnov's taxi came to a stop, in the upper eighties. The Phantom's cab stopped at a discreet distance behind. Van leaned forward. He saw the figure of Count Karnov alight to the curb, pay off his driver, then stride beneath the canopy of a towering apartment building.

Swiftly, Van paid off his own cabby and moved to the canopy of the apartment. Karnov's figure had already disappeared into the building.

The Phantom pushed in through the glass-paned doors. His alert eyes flashed around a large, ornate foyer. Three elevators stood with gates open, but a smaller bronze door was closed. From behind it the Phantom's keen ears heard the sound of mechanical motion. A private elevator in such a building invariably led to a penthouse.

That was where the desperate Count Karnov was apparently going.

The Phantom paused a moment in a manner which befitted his vacuous expression before he walked into one of the regular elevators-first glancing up at the last number on the indicator.

"Twenty-eight," he said to the operator, as the gates slid smoothly shut and the car began its swift ascent.

The elevator took him to the top floor of the apartment. He sauntered out, in a leisurely manner. But as soon as the gates had closed behind him, his leisure dropped away like a cloak. Moving swiftly, he found the fire-stairs, and ascended to the penthouse floor. As he climbed, he slipped on his domino mask.

Emerging on a landing, a skylight overhead showing the gathering twilight, he saw the closed bronzed door of the private elevator, the door opposite to the only apartment up here.

He slipped to it on soundless feet. He put his face close to it, listened. He heard a vague sound within. Then a voice. He could only catch a few words, but those were enough to sharpen the gleam in his eyes.

"—a transatlantic call-to London, England-reverse the charges-hurry —"

Karnov's voice!

A tight, grim smile flecked Van's lips. The pieces of this mighty, bloody puzzle were clicking into place; he knew that he was close now to the end of the gruesome trail. But many threads were still loose, many questions still to answer.

The penthouse lock was difficult, especially difficult to open without sound. His wire twisted, curved, wriggled in and out, as his deft hand guided it.

At last it clicked. The Phantom turned the handle slowly. Cautiously, he pushed the door open. Its well-oiled hinges made no sound. Wraith-like, he slipped into the apartment. A wide stucco-walled hall, deep in unlit twilight gloom, engulfed his stealthy figure. His keen eyes flashed down the hall. Two doors, one on either side of the wall opposite the entrance door. Which?

A sharp ring of a telephone answered his question in the next second. He heard a quick, leaping step in the phone room. Karnov's voice was speaking.

"Hello? Yes-my party? Yes, I'm holding on —"

The Phantom moved to the door, peered in, cautiously. The room was in gloom, no lights having been lit. Twilight showed outside a single open window that evidently was flush, on this side, with the building —a sheer drop into space. The room itself, a living room, looked strangely feminine in its appearance. Soft, silky covered furniture. And a faint perfumed scent.

At a taboret to one side, Count Karnov crouched over a white-enameled telephone. His voice came again in its flawless English.

"Hello-This is Karnov!" Anger threaded that voice now. "Listen to me! I have reached the end of my rope! I intend to leave this country at once." He laughed harshly. "Oh, I got enough money. I have done as much of my work as I could —"

The Phantom, his ears taking in every word, had slipped into the room behind Count Karnov.

Like a panther, the Phantom leaped! His right hand closed on Karnov's hand holding the telephone. His left hand stifled the amazed out-cry on the Count's lips.

He twisted the phone out of Karnov's fingers, managed to place the instrument down-still out of its cradle.

His right hand, now free, doubled into a balled fist. It did not move far; but it moved with timed precision and judgment. The blow landed on the Count's bristle-bearded jaw. The foreigner staggered backwards, his mouth open now and unhampered, but only an expelling sigh coming from it. He slumped in the shadowy gloom of the far wall.

The Phantom, deciding he was out for the time being, did not delay another instant. He grabbed up the phone. Immediately an angry voice came to his ears.

"Are you there, Karnov? Confound you! Why don't you answer?"

Van felt a thrill in that hectic moment. He was listening to a voice that was coming from three thousand miles-across the Atlantic Ocean-from England.

"Yes, I am here," Van said into the mouthpiece, speaking in the flawless voice of Count Karnov. "Listen to me. You have read, doubtless, the newspapers. The detective called the Phantom is working upon this case. He is ready, almost, to bring it to a close!" Though he spoke in Karnov's voice, his words rang with grim sincerity now, for they were true words. "He needs but one more proof! You must act swiftly if you wish to save yourself! I have already told you what I am going to do! But you must make a sacrifice!"

"Karnov!" the English-accented voice rose harshly. "What do you mean? What do you dare to —?"

"You must come to America, to New York, at once!" Van went on. "Take now the fastest boat! One perhaps with a mail-service plane-charter it if you can! That will bring you in the more swiftly!"

"Karnov, are you mad? Are you trying to make me put my head into a noose? Here I am, safe with a perfect alibi —" As if realizing he had said too much over the public wire, the speaker broke off with a gasp. "You are mad!" he finished weakly.

"I warn you for your own good. It is a matter of life and death," Van said, with difficulty keeping the voice of Karnov. "The Phantom will get to you, regardless —" He went on speaking, rapidly, persuasively.

He heard a movement behind him then. He jerked back his head quickly, expecting to see Karnov getting to his feet. His eyes went wide then, as he stifled a surprised exclamation. Karnov was not in the twilight room at all! He had vanished! And instead —

"Put down that telephone!" came a steady, low feminine voice.

In the doorway of the room stood the slender, white-faced figure of the missing Queen Stella! A small but deadly automatic gleamed dully in her hand.

Her eyes gleaming with a determined light, the girl aerialist advanced towards the telephone as she spoke.

The Phantom spoke three hurried words more into the mouthpiece in that split second. "Get here quick!" Then he banged the phone down in its cradle, and leaped upright, whirling toward the girl. He saw her finger tighten on the trigger-and his body sprang as if from a catapult.

His long right arm snaked out, catching the gun as flame spat from it, twisting it so the bullet was deflected to one side. Simultaneously he saw the girl's eyes widen with horror and astonishment, realized she was staring in the gloom at his domino mask.

A cry of relief came to her lips, but even as she opened her mouth to speak, there was a rush of heavy feet from the hall. Like a flood, slouch-hatted figures burst into the room with leveled guns!

The remainder of the Fang's mob! Led by the slicker-clad Monk Gorman!

The girl screamed. Van grabbed her by the arm, half flung her across the room, where she dropped under the window. He still had the automatic he had twisted out of her hand. He pivoted, swinging it upon the charging mob of gunmen and jerking the trigger.

Crack! A thug dropped in his tracks —a pimply-faced man whose life blood spurted from his chest as he fell. Monk Gorman, moving rapidly despite his size, reached the light switch.

The room became dazzling with the sudden flood of illumination. Before the blinking Van could fire again, the thugs were upon him. There were enough of them to make resistance futile. He was pummeled, cuffed, kicked, by hate-glaring felons of the underworld!

Stunned, he was pushed back across the floor. As he fought to keep his balance, he heard a faint moan beside him. Queen Stella standing there, all blood drained from her face.

Both of them, unarmed, were facing a line of thugs who stood between them and the door. Guns were leveling at the two captives. Monk, in their center, holding the deadliest weapon of all, a blue-steel tommy gun, at which he had already proved himself adept!

"Well, well!" he chortled above its barrel. "This time we really got you where we want you, Phantom! Got you lined up, an' you, too, Sister!" His evil eyes swiveled to the girl.

Outside in the hall, beyond the closed door of this room, sounded a step. Another person had entered the apartment, was walking down that hall!

The steps came forward decisively, entered the room next to the living room where all were listening breathlessly.

The connecting door opened just a few inches. Blackness only showed from within. But once more, as he had felt in that ghastly studio at Astoria, Van was aware in every nerve of a blighting evil Presence!

The menace he knew as the Fang had followed to this penthouse apartment, trapping him there. The next instant a familiar, rasping voice sounded from that chinked door.

"So, Mr. Phantom, you have crossed my trail again!" A diabolical chortle rose from the darkness beyond the ajar door. "We have caught two birds, as it were! One who is just a foolish young woman. The other devilishly clever-and of many lives, it seems. I suppose, if I were to have Monk remove your silly domino, I would see the features of Al Millett this time. Bah! Your childish disguises weary me. But your escapes annoy me. This time I'll watch you die with my own eyes!"

Van was silent, eyes fixed on the door. The girl stood just behind him at the window, pale, yet with a certain defiance on her delicate, oval face. From her lips came a low whisper which barely reached the Phantom's ears.

"I'm sorry," she murmured. "I didn't know it was you. I sent Karnov for the police while you were talking over the phone. I thought you were the Fang. And all I've done is to help trap you —"

Van broke in quickly. "I know, Miss Millett," he said simply, sympathy and understanding in his tone.

"What are you saying, Phantom?" came the evil voice from the other room where the terrible genius behind this whole bloody reign of crime stood in darkness. "You speak? You had better finish swiftly. The boys are waiting."

Which was unpleasantly true. Monk's blue-steel tommy gun was raised, ready. The other thugs formed a line of dark, hungry automatic muzzles. The Phantom remained stoically silent. He was thinking furiously.

"Come, come," mocked the arch criminal. "Do you not wish to talk before you die? It is a boon I grant you-both of you. You aren't gagged. You seem to know so much, to be so astute. Talk your way out of this impasse, Mr. Phantom."

"You fiend!" exclaimed the girl vehemently. "You inhuman —"

"Steady," counseled the Phantom, flashing a glance at her.

She fell silent. And Van Loan's eyes continued to rove swiftly about the room. If it were not for the girl, he might have found some means of escape. But at the first move, even if he managed to win clear, those guns would blast, and the girl would die. And it was very essential now that this girl did not die. If only he could stall until the police came!

The window! A sheer drop, with nothing but flimsy ledges to hold to. It would take an acrobat-Into his mind flashed the swinging trapeze at the Palladium Club. He reached in that moment the most desperate decision of his career.

He glanced quickly at the girl and then let his gaze dart toward the open window behind her.

"Dare you?" he whispered tersely out of the corner of his mouth.

She understood instantly. Her eyes widened, sparkled.

"Yes," she formed with her lips.

"So you won't talk, eh?" grated the voice from the other room, mockingly imitating a third-grade detective. "Well, too bad you won't live to file this case —"

"Wait!" said Van Loan sharply. "I'll talk."

"I'm listening," agreed the unseen man amiably. "What have you to say?"

"This!" shot out the Phantom, without warning hurling himself down and sideways straight at the waiting line of gangsters.

Before they could react, before they could train their weapons upon him, he was tangled against the legs of three of them. With a mighty sweep, he gathered legs and all within reach to himself, and brought the amazed thugs to the floor in a mad scramble with him.

"Sit down on him!" barked the vindictive voice of the hidden leader. "Fools! The girl! Grab her!"

But it was too late. Like a sleek jungle cat, Queen Stella had swung herself up into the window at the Phantom's first move, and out into the nothingness of space. Guns roared futilely, hot lead smacking into the window frame, shattering the upper sash, and drumming out into the open air.

Monk Gorman and two of his muscle men yanked the Phantom savagely to his feet, while others darted over to the window and gawked out into the night, seeing nothing but the myriad winking lights of New York skyscrapers.

"Gawd! She's gone, Chief!" gasped one. "She did a Brodie!"

"Her body'll attract attention, Boss!" shouted Gorman. "We better finish this guy an' lam."

"Wait!" snarled the leader. "This building is recessed. She didn't fall to the street. We'll have time. I want you to search this place."

"Anyway, this guy ain't gonna die like that," grunted Monk Gorman viciously, and he crashed the muzzle of his tommy gun against the head of the Phantom.

The world exploded for Van Loan, and he went out like a light. Went out, crumpling to the floor, just as the entrance door of the apartment crashed back against the wall, and the charging rush of heavy feet surged like a wave into the penthouse.

"Th' cops!" howled a panic-stricken thug. "Scram, everybody!"

"You can't scram," snarled the unseen leader. "Fight it out, you scum! You're trapped and done for if you don't!"

Pandemonium reigned. Through the hallway door came the charge of bluecoats. Guns barked their snarls of defiance. Smoke filled the room with the reek of cordite. Men bowled over like ten-pins, screaming in agony. Gangsters and policemen in one mad carnage of hell!

The end was inevitable. Monk Gorman, his machine gun chattering like an enraged ape, took a slug over the heart just as his stream of leaden hail cut an officer almost in two. His gun went silent as he grunted once and dropped to the floor, his career of crime over forever. The remnants of four mobs had met their Waterloo.

The police were busily mopping up when Queen Stella and Count Karnov pushed their way in. The girl uttered a cry of alarm at sight of the Phantom on the floor, and rushed to his side. He was already stirring, conscious again as she raised his head.

A plainclothes detective rushed in from the recently darkened room and reported to Inspector Gregg who was in charge of this raid, having been found at Milady's Salon by the frenzied Karnov.

"Inspector," he babbled, "there was a murdered man in that bedroom as I went through a minute ago-lying on the floor in the dark with his neck broken. I saw it! Head twisted nastily to one side, tongue hanging out. I went on to the kitchen with the harness bulls to make sure everything was mopped up, and then I came back to examine the corpse-and it was gone!"

"You're nuts, O'Brien," snapped Inspector Gregg curtly. "If—"

The Phantom pushed away Queen Stella's fluttering hands and staggered erect. He reeled his dizzy way into the room in question. It was empty!

He came back to the living room doorway, catching on to the casing for support. A bitter smile twisted his mouth beneath his awry mask.

"On the contrary, inspector," he said wearily, "O'Brien is not nuts."

"Then, maybe I am," growled Gregg acidly. "I found out, too late, about that tricky vase at the restaurant. It's rigged up like lots of those European places —a blind for a clothes chute to the cellar for soiled napkins and tablecloths."

Had he not been so intensely disappointed, Van Loan could have laughed.

"I know," he articulated wearily. "But this dead man with the broken neck was a better trick. That was no dead man. *He was the master criminal!* And we've let him get away!"

Chapter XV
The Phantom Speaks

Five days later the big room on the third floor of Police Headquarters on Centre Street held a queer group of people. Besides the commissioner, Inspector Gregg, and half a dozen uniformed officers, there were numerous visitors.

Frank Havens, the publisher, was there at the desk with a mass of papers before him. Seated in a semi-circle facing the desk were four well-known figures of the amusement world-Paul Corbin, Gordon Drake, John Gifford, and Carl Fenwick.

"I don't understand," said Paul Corbin nervously, "why we are all gathered here like this. We've been waiting half an hour. And for what?" He seemed more womanish than ever in his pettish annoyance.

Gordon Drake clasped his gloved hands stiffly, a tolerant smile about his handsome lips. "Contain yourself, my dear Corbin," he advised.

"Nobody's been killed during the past five days, anyhow. That's something."

John Gifford merely grunted. His big frame seemed more huddled than usual, his craggy, gnarled features more grotesque than ever.

Fenwick said nothing. He merely tapped on the arms of his chair, tugged at his high collar, tweaked at his ear, and went back to his drumming.

Inspector Gregg shuffled through some papers at his own desk, scowled at his assorted company, and squinted at the calm and composed publisher of the *Clarion*.

"I'm getting a bit impatient, myself," he said gruffly. "The Phantom asked for this meeting, promising to break this Fang case for us today. And he isn't even here. What's the answer, Mr. Havens?"

The grey-haired publisher smiled as he looked up from the papers he was carefully arranging.

"I can't explain, inspector," he admitted frankly. "All I can tell you is that the Phantom has promised to meet us here and surprise us. And he never breaks a promise. As for these papers, he'll have to tell us exactly what they mean."

An orderly came in and spoke to the police commissioner. The latter cleared his throat and glanced around the group. Then "Send him in," he said.

All eyes turned to the door as the orderly went out. In an instant another figure appeared on the threshold. And four men gasped in amazement. A young man with buck teeth, thick lips, and attired in the quaint garb of the first decade of the twentieth century looked over the company, smiled, and came forward.

"Hello, Gordon, Carl, Paul, John," he greeted. "You remember me?"

Paul Corbin half-rose out of his chair with a stifled scream.

"Al Millett!" he choked, eyes bulging in terror.

"Don't be a fool!" growled John Gifford. "Al Millett looks as old as we do today."

"True," smiled Gordon Drake. "This is the ghost of Al Millett of yesterday. Hello, Al."

"This is crazy!" snorted Fenwick, tugging at his collar.

Inspector Gregg was on his feet, hesitating in pardonable uncertainty.

"You are all correct and all wrong, gentlemen," smiled the newcomer, approaching the desk and taking up a position beside the publisher and the pile of papers. "I am neither Al Millett, nor the bloody criminal called the Fang. This was just a screwy idea of my own. A great many people know me as-the Phantom. I'm sorry to have kept you waiting, but I had to meet a boat —a different one from the *Charlemagne*. Allow me to present the real Albert Millett!"

At his words, almost before the various gasps of surprise died away, another man crossed the threshold, a middle-aged man on whose arm came the aerialist known as Queen Stella.

The newcomer, a pleasant-faced man with greying hair and thick lips about which there were deep lines, came forward hesitantly and bowed stiffly in English fashion.

For a full moment there was a stunned silence. Then Inspector Gregg started forward with a growl.

"Wait, please!" crisped the Phantom. "Albert Millett, where have you been for the past twenty years?"

"I have been in the wine business in London," answered Millett. "I was a fool as a young man out West, and, after my wife died, I went away with my daughter to start life anew. This is my daughter, Estella Millett. She has been in America for more than a year. She inherited her mother's ability as an aerialist, and that has become her chosen calling."

"When, Mr. Millett, did you arrive in America?" inquired the Phantom, making no effort to conceal the fact that this was a rehearsed inquiry.

"I set foot on my native land for the first time in twenty years just an hour ago when the *Queen Mary* docked," replied Millett in a firm voice.

"You can establish this fact?" went on the Phantom coolly.

"Without question. I left England but four days ago."

"Then you couldn't possibly have landed from the *Charlemagne* a week ago in New York?"

"I could not, sir."

"Then you could not be this fiendish murderer who has terrorized New York for the past week under the name of the Fang?"

"Most certainly not!" said Millett emphatically.

"Then this," cut in Inspector Gregg succinctly, "shoots our case all to hell, and we're back where we started from. I thought you were going to break it, Phantom."

"I'll have to go into it methodically," answered the Phantom. "I'll try to be brief, inspector. By the way, Count Karnov-as you have already ascertained-is Mr. Millett's representative in the United States. He is exactly what he purports to be, and no more. As for breaking the Fang case-let me explain that Mr. Havens and I have had to dig back into a lot of ancient history. For one thing, the Academy of Medicine had to canvass a great part of the United States for us in search of certain knowledge. We have dug up a number of interesting family skeletons.

"First, I might touch on the once famous circus of Crowley and Buckill wherewith Al Millett got his bad exploitation as a fanged monster. There are handbills and circus posters here that will interest you, Inspector Gregg. But the private life of Al Millett has little bearing on this case. He was just a red herring dragged across this trail. The real criminal is not Millett, nor his daughter, nor Karnov, nor anybody imported into this country. He is one of the very men, inspector, who came to you with that wild tale about the Fang."

The inspector gasped. "You mean that yarn was made out of whole cloth? One of them was the maniac? Andrews! By God, it is Andrews! The missing man!"

"Not so fast, inspector," the Phantom calmed him. "I'll tell you. But first —" He turned toward the tense and alert four tycoons of the entertainment world. " —before I can clear up the matter, I must ask your permission, gentlemen, to reveal jealously guarded secrets of your intimate life. It pains me to embarrass you, but the truth will have to come out. You know what I refer to-the Gargoyle Club."

All four men winced. Paul Corbin, unaccountably, began to sob. Gifford seemed to shrink in his chair, growing more crag-like than ever. Fenwick turned deadly pale. Gordon Drake was the first to recover. He laughed bitterly and stood erect, stretching his manly figure to its full, symmetric height.

"After all," he said wearily, "why not? Nature made us what we are. It's nothing to be personally ashamed of."

"Thank you," said the Phantom softly. "I respect you, Mr. Drake. These brutal and revolting murders, each different, were not the haphazard affairs that you may think, Inspector Gregg-Commissioner. They were perfectly logical when one knows the reason. Had they continued, they would have woven the same grotesque pattern of startling individuality. For instance, Drake-had he been killed-would have been found with his arms amputated at the shoulders. Paul Corbin's body would have been split in half.

"Gifford would have been horribly mangled-as he so nearly was by his own Leap-for-Life railway. And Carl Fenwick —*would have been found with a broken neck!*"

At these last emphatic words, Fenwick leaped to his feet with a strangled cry. In a flash Van Loan had him covered with a pistol, his face set in hard, uncompromising lines which almost revealed the clean-cut contour of the face of Richard Van Loan.

"Hold it, Fenwick!" he said, cold steel in his voice. "Take him, Inspector Gregg! He is your man!"

The inspector, though dumbfounded, was a good policeman. Without question he leaped forward and snapped a pair of manacles about the theatrical producer's wrists. Two uniformed officers converged on the accused man and gripped his arms. Fenwick wilted.

"But-but just what does this all mean?" demanded the confused commissioner.

"Just this, sir," answered the Phantom. "Nine men, today wealthy and famous, were once freaks in the show of Crowley and Buckill. In those days when hokum was king, these genuine freaks were featured attractions. They laid the foundations of their own fortunes while they made Crowley and Buckill rich.

"The Marcy brothers were Siamese twins, joined together by a cartilage and a spinal structure. An operation might have severed them, but both were afraid to chance it. When they retired from circus life they became recluses, exhibiting themselves only behind a double desk or in their limousine. They were always together, of course, hampered by their natal tie, but remarkable business men for all of that."

Van Loan drew a breath and continued.

"Clyde Dickson was a different sort of oddity. He was not born with his affliction. As a young man on a construction job a flying crowbar was driven into his skull. By some queer accident it didn't kill him. So it was sawed off and left in his head. There is another case of this nature on record at the Harvard Medical School. They have the skull of a man whose name was Gage. He was injured like Dickson, and lived to die normally at an old age.

"I have the record here of Dickson's case, the report of the son of the doctor who waited on him. That was why Dickson wore a mop of long hair over the protuberance from his skull.

"Meade, the fourth man to die, was another extraordinary case. At some time in his early life he developed a stricture of his esophagus which prevented him from taking food. He was operated on, an artificial opening was made at the front of his throat, and he lived. He exhibited this second mouth as a freak in the circus.

"Andrews has not run away. He is dead. His case is one where his torso developed normally, but his legs from the hips down atrophied as a child. I saw those severed legs in that abandoned studio out in Astoria. He wore special braces and used a cane, if you will remember.

"You see, each murder had to be different in order to obliterate the fact that the victims were abnormal or subnormal. Gifford would have been mutilated because he is a hunch-back. I found that out when I saved him from his own rocket car. He was phenomenally light; his padded clothes partially hiding his deformity and giving him a portly appearance.

"Paul Corbin is half man and half woman, a genuine hermaphrodite. Gordon Drake was born without any forearms, the upper arms ending in stubs about the elbow, stubs that he learned to handle so dexterously that he was one of the most interesting attractions of the circus."

"I did better with them than I ever have with these artificial arms," admitted Drake ruefully.

"Fenwick was another queer experiment of nature," went on the Phantom. "One vertebra in his neck is missing. Instead, he has a section of limber cartilage. He is able to dislocate his neck and assume the appearance of a man with a broken neck at will. That is why he always wears a high, stiff collar.

"And that completes our group of unusual men, men so bizarre that they felt they had no place in normal life. So they remained banded together, forming a little club of their own which they called the Gargoyle Club and where they could be at ease and at rest, where nobody stared or commented on the infirmity or deformity of another."

"But why did Fenwick go berserk?" demanded Gregg.

"All their holdings were pooled," explained the Phantom. "All their wealth was in a holding corporation which was licensed under the name of the Star Corporation. They supported charitable institutions for afflicted persons. Upon their several deaths, the estate was to go into such endowments.

"But Fenwick was the exception. Instead of pitying others, he was intensely bitter-and he was the least afflicted of the lot. Since he couldn't inherit from the others, he undertook to murder and rob them.

"The thwarted armored truck holdup would have been his sweetest haul. He must have planned his bloody crimes for years. I doubt if he knew Al Millett was still alive until Dickson gave Estella Millett a job at the Palladium Club. And that only intensified matters, because Fenwick was a disappointed suitor for the hand of Estella's mother.

"I think I was about the last person to hear Andrews's voice. I surprised Fenwick with him at the Gargoyle Club the night he was killed, and when I so nearly was. And, gentlemen, I think that about winds up the most bizarre case I have ever had the pleasure of assisting the Homicide Bureau with. We all owe a great deal of thanks to Mr. Frank Havens for his painstaking research and finding of old records."

"Which reminds me of one thing," spoke up the publisher. "How did my cartoonist, Collins, get mixed up in this business?"

"That was an unfortunate accident," said the Phantom. "He was a very inquisitive and aggressive young chap. He was acquainted with Estella Millett, who knew of these men from her father. One night in an unguarded moment, she let something slip about fact being stranger than fiction. She mentioned the names of Dickson and Marcy, and that was all Collins needed. He ferreted out enough to seal his own doom.

"What puzzled me for a long time was how the leader of the crime gang always knew I escaped from his death traps before he should have known. That was the first clue which led to Fenwick. Fenwick kept in touch with the Phantom through Mr. Havens, and that smartness was finally instrumental in bringing about his downfall."

Carl Fenwick raised his head and stared at the Phantom with hate-glazed eyes. Then, uttering a mad cry of bafflement, he tore free from the laxly guarding officers and rushed straight toward the nearest window. Heedless of the shouts behind him, he dove head first through the glass.

When those with sufficient hardihood gained the window and looked down, they saw uniformed police running to surround the ghastly remains of the most horrible Gargoyle.

By an irony of fate, Carl Fenwick had actually broken his neck in his fall.

"I am truly sorry for you all," said the Phantom wearily. "I only hope you who are left are able to pick up your lives and go on bravely from here. As for me —" His broad shoulders drooped with fatigue. " —I think I'll retire to the shades and sleep for a week."

They watched him depart in awed silence. Only Frank Havens knew the full extent of the suffering the Phantom had borne, and his heart swelled at the thought of the man who had dedicated his wealth and his life to protect and safeguard his fellow men from crime while the careless world little suspected that the rich idler, Richard Curtis Van Loan, was the Phantom who troubled the dreams of criminals.

www.ingramcontent.com/pod-product-compliance
Lightning Source LLC
Chambersburg PA
CBHW070807120626
46557CB00002B/752